Three women. Three fantasies.

Years ago Gemma, Zoe and Violet all took the same college sex-ed class, one they laughingly referred to as Sex for Beginners. It was an easy credit—not something they'd ever need in real life. Or so they thought...

Their professor had them each write a letter, outlining their most private, most outrageous sexual fantasies. They never dreamed their letters would be returned to them when they least expected it. Or that their own words would change their lives forever...

Don't miss Stephanie Bond's newest miniseries:

Sex for Beginners

WATCH AND LEARN
(October 2008)

IN A BIND
(November 2008)

NO PEEKING...
(December 2008)

Sex for Beginners
What you don't know...might turn you on!

Blaze™

Dear Reader,

Have you ever run across an old childhood diary or a note you wrote in high school or college? It can be fun, and even revealing, to see what you were thinking when you were younger, what things were important to you.

The seniors at Women's Covington College who took the Sexual Psyche class (dubbed by the students as "Sex for Beginners") were given an assignment to write down their innermost sexual fantasies in the form of a letter to themselves. Their letter was to be cataloged with a code for anonymity and remain sealed for ten years, then mailed to them.

Violet Summerlin, uptight owner of a personal concierge business, receives her letter just before Christmas, her busiest time of year. Yet the naughty words she wrote give her pause—she hasn't experienced exciting out-of-the-bedroom sex as she'd fantasized. So when her best client, a sexy extreme-sports junkie, invites her to Miami for a working vacation, she accepts—with adrenaline-pumping results!

I hope you enjoy *No Peeking...*, the third book in the SEX FOR BEGINNERS trilogy. Please tell your friends about the wonderful stories you find between the pages of Harlequin novels! And visit me at www.stephaniebond.com.

Happy endings always,

Stephanie Bond

STEPHANIE BOND

No Peeking...

TORONTO • NEW YORK • LONDON
AMSTERDAM • PARIS • SYDNEY • HAMBURG
STOCKHOLM • ATHENS • TOKYO • MILAN • MADRID
PRAGUE • WARSAW • BUDAPEST • AUCKLAND

Recycling programs
for this product may
not exist in your area.

ISBN-13: 978-0-373-79444-7
ISBN-10: 0-373-79444-4

NO PEEKING...

www.eHarlequin.com

Printed in U.S.A.

ABOUT THE AUTHOR

Stephanie Bond thinks the world would be a better place if only more people read romance novels! "My goal," says Stephanie, "is to leave readers with a smile and a sigh." To date, Stephanie has written more than forty romance and mystery novels, and doesn't plan on slowing down anytime soon at what she considers to be "her dream job." Stephanie lives in midtown Atlanta with her hunky architect/artist/hero husband.

Books by Stephanie Bond

HARLEQUIN BLAZE
2—TWO SEXY!
169—MY FAVORITE MISTAKE
282—JUST DARE ME…
338—SHE DID A BAD,
    BAD THING
428—WATCH AND LEARN
434—IN A BIND

HARLEQUIN TEMPTATION
685—MANHUNTING
    IN MISSISSIPPI
718—CLUB CUPID
751—ABOUT LAST NIGHT…
769—IT TAKES A REBEL
805—SEEKING SINGLE MALE
964—COVER ME

MIRA BOOKS
BODY MOVERS
BODY MOVERS:
  2 BODIES FOR THE PRICE OF 1
BODY MOVERS:
  3 MEN AND A BODY

Don't miss any of our special offers. Write to us at the following address for information on our newest releases.

Harlequin Reader Service
U.S.: 3010 Walden Ave., P.O. Box 1325, Buffalo, NY 14269
Canadian: P.O. Box 609, Fort Erie, Ont. L2A 5X3

For Chris, who still gets my heart pumping.

1

Six days until Christmas

"WHAT YOU NEED IS something warm and cuddly for Christmas."

Violet Summerlin frowned into the cell phone she juggled on her shoulder, even though her friend Nan couldn't see her. "I told you, I'm way too busy for a pet." Then she looked down at the fluffy butterscotch-colored Pekingese she was walking in the park. "My own, anyway."

Nan's sigh sounded over the line. "I was talking about a man."

"No time for one of those, either," Violet quipped.

"You work way too hard. When are you going to start delegating things to your new assistant? Wasn't that the idea of hiring her?"

Violet chewed on her lower lip. "I'm still feeling out Lillian. She's nice, but her working style is different than mine."

"You mean she isn't anal retentive? Maybe this Lillian will help you to loosen up."

"Christmas is one of my busiest times of the year. I can't afford to loosen up right now."

"Violet," Nan said softly, "it might not be such a bad idea to slow down. Since you lost your grandparents…I don't know. You seem wound even tighter than usual."

"I miss them terribly," Violet confessed. "Even with Mom and Dad back in town, sometimes I just feel so…lost."

"I know, sweetie, but the hours that you work— it's not healthy. You're going to wake up one day and wish you'd indulged in a misspent youth."

Violet stopped abruptly as the pooch came up short on the leash, wrinkling his little pug face. Winslow, the Pekingese, looked up at her and barked, a sharp noise that sounded like fabric ripping.

"Thanks for the advice, Nan, but I have to run. The dog won't go if I'm on the phone."

"You're kidding, right?"

"No. He's a spoiled little thing and has to have my undivided attention to…you know."

"I would laugh except I know old lady Kingsbury is probably paying you a fortune to do her bidding."

"I'm a personal concierge, Nan. I do whatever my clients need me to do."

"Especially that yummy Dominick Burns."

Nan's favorite subject was Violet's best customer, who also happened to be the most notorious playboy in Atlanta. She ignored the little spike in her own pulse—she'd harbored a secret crush on the man for almost a year. "Until I'm successful enough to pick and choose my clients, I guess I have to put up with all kinds of animals," she said lightly.

"Yeah, but no one's going to get that man on a leash." Nan was panting harder than Winslow.

"Is that the best you can come up with today?" Violet asked, her voice deadpan.

"No wonder his last name is Burns. The man is positively flammable, a four-alarm fire, burn me up and hose me down—"

"Good grief, woman, go take a cold shower." Violet disconnected the call, cutting off Nan's laughter, then squatted down to face Winslow, nose to snout.

"Okay, I'm all yours. Now, will you please do your business?"

The dog emitted a chastising little bark and angled his head.

Violet sighed, then glanced at her watch and caved like a wall of ice cream. Time was money, after all.

"You're such a good boy," she cooed in her best baby voice, petting his arrogant little head. "Yes, you are. You're such a pretty, good boy. Yes, you are."

Satisfied, Winslow assumed the position and Violet looked away with a wince.

Some days she questioned her decision to open Summerlin at Your Service, and this was one of those days—it had been an unending stream of tedious trips to the dry cleaners to pick up and drop off shirts, to courier offices to pack and send parcels, and to Patricia Kingsbury's house to walk her contrary pet, Winslow, who pushed the boundaries of his breed's reputation for willful and jealous behavior.

Luckily, most clients preferred to pay Violet's premium fees to do things that were more productive, such as setting up a wireless network for their computer or decorating their house for the holidays. Raised by a grandfather who was an electronics and mechanical whiz and a grandmother who could give Martha Stewart a run for her money, Violet had honed her varied abilities with a masters in business administration and five years in the hospitality industry working assorted jobs, from customer service to operations. Since starting her concierge business three years ago, she prided herself on not having yet received a request from a client that she couldn't fulfill.

Then she frowned. Except the times when the flirtatious Dominick Burns had hinted he wouldn't mind a little *personal* attention from Violet.

The devilishly handsome bad boy who'd made a fortune designing and manufacturing extreme sports gear was too busy to handle day-to-day details, but he'd told her he didn't like the thought of having an entourage of people on the payroll to tend to him. So Violet stopped by his office once a week to pick up a to-do list that might consist of anything from selecting a suit for him to wear to a special occasion, to selecting personal stationery, to buying a gift for his latest girlfriend.

She wondered wryly what his various and sundry women would think if they knew that the man hadn't walked the aisles of local boutiques to find the perfect gift for their three-date anniversary or whatever the made-up occasion that was no doubt meant to unhinge the women's legs.

But the man was generous, Violet conceded. And he usually had interesting and challenging assignments for her, many of which had put her on the fringe of his business activities. Her pulse ticked higher as she wondered what she'd discover on his agenda today. With only a week until Christmas, it seemed likely that he would hand over his gift list. Mentally scrolling through the women for whom she'd bought gifts throughout the year, she came up with an estimate of twenty.

A nice, round number, she thought wryly.

She leaned over to bag Winslow's offering, deposited it in a nearby trash can and urged him in the direction of his home. The air carried a chill and she wondered if by some miracle she would see snow for

Christmas. Even in the dead of winter, snow in Atlanta was rare. But she could hope.

Sadly, this would be her first year without her grandparents. But her somewhat elusive parents had taken a break from their world travels to stay in her grandparents' house for a while and spend the holidays with Violet. She missed Grammy and Gramps desperately, but she'd always dreamed of sharing a magical Christmas with her parents when she was young. Still, it had never been more than a dream. Her mother and father were simply too wrapped up in each other to pay their daughter much mind.

But now that she could orchestrate the holiday herself, she was eagerly anticipating the three of them sipping hot cider around an ornament-laden tree, with the aroma of a ham in the oven, and carols in the background as they exchanged heartfelt, meaningful gifts to express their love for each other. She had made her mother a coverlet out of her grandmother's house dresses and had bought her father a beautiful set of hand tools for the workshop he'd been talking about setting up in the garage. After years away, flitting around the globe for her father's job as a translator to diplomats, it seemed as if her parents were finally settling down.

Violet sighed in contentment. It would be the best Christmas ever.

A half block away from the Kingsbury house, a

towering brick structure draped with holiday lights that Violet herself had installed, Winslow jutted out his little underbite, then sat down.

And refused to budge.

Irritated, Violet scooped him up and carried him the rest of the way. Which was, she realized as he pressed his cold nose to her shoulder, exactly what he'd wanted her to do, the little beast.

"You're incorrigible," she chastised.

Patricia Kingsbury met them at the door to take Winslow into her bejeweled arms. The dog stiffened, but went, even though he looked back at Violet and whined.

"Did he go poo-poo?" Patricia sounded concerned, but her face remained expressionless, which Violet attributed to the woman's regular BOTOX injections.

"Er…yes."

Patricia cuddled her poufy dog. "You always seem to know how to make him go, Violet."

"It's a gift," Violet agreed. "If there's nothing else, Ms. Kingsbury—"

"Violet, you've worked for me for two years. Please call me Patricia."

"Patricia," Violet amended with a smile, "if there's nothing else—"

"I put my grocery list on the table. And would you mind taking a few things back to the mall for me, dear?" She pointed to a mound of bags on a settee.

"Not at all."

"Here's my credit card. Just have everything reversed and if there are any problems, call me."

"I'm sure there won't be any problems," Violet said pleasantly, then gathered the list and the bags in her arms and waddled toward the door. "I'll drop off your credit card tomorrow morning."

"Tomorrow afternoon is fine, dear, when you come back to walk Winslow. He'll be ready to toodle again by then."

Violet maintained her smile. "Great. See you then."

Being relegated to a dog coach wasn't so bad, she told herself as she steered her hybrid SUV onto I-75 northbound. Ms. Kingsbury rarely had difficult requests, and she'd given Violet many referrals. With this job, one learned to take the bad with the good.

After battling six lanes of traffic for thirty minutes, Violet reached a subdivision where three empty upscale houses were for sale. She'd been commissioned to go through and knock down cobwebs, adjust the temperature, put fresh flowers in vases and generally ensure that when an agent stopped by with a potential customer, there were no surprises—such as the bankrupted former owner of the house living in a closet. Or a raccoon in the kitchen. Or a fallen tree sticking through the bedroom ceiling.

She'd seen it all.

Armed with Gerbera daisies, a broom and a Taser,

she sped through the houses, opening doors and checking every nook and cranny. After an uneventful sweep, she jumped on I-75 southbound and fought traffic again to reach a tobacco store, where she picked up the box of cigars she'd special-ordered for Dominick Burns last week, then turned her car toward her office in midtown. A few blocks away her cell phone rang. It was Lillian. Hoping nothing was wrong, Violet touched the hands-free microphone on her visor. "Hi, Lillian, what's up?"

"You have a visitor. Dominick Burns?"

Violet frowned. "I'm scheduled to stop by his office in Buckhead this afternoon for our weekly conference."

"He said he was in the area and that he'd wait." Lillian lowered her voice. "He's rather handsome. And he asked for a vodka tonic."

Violet rolled her eyes. "I don't have a bar in my office. Get him a cup of coffee and I'll be there in five minutes."

She checked her hair and makeup in the mirror, telling herself she'd do the same for any client. She smoothed a couple of errant hairs that had escaped her standard neat ponytail—the ponytail that Dominick Burns teased her about. Her black pantsuit also was standard, with a white shirt that changed with the season—nice T-shirts for spring, sleeveless shells for summer, three-quarter-length sleeves in fall, and a turtleneck for winter. She had already moved into her turtleneck drawer. Comfortable black loafers completed the look that allowed her to blend in almost anywhere. Her "uniform" wasn't as glamorous as what Dominick's girlfriends probably wore, but she looked professional, and that was all that mattered.

It wasn't as if Dominick was interested in her.

Violet wheeled into the parking garage and pulled into one of the four spots assigned to her live/work condo, with its tiny storefront on the first level that faced Juniper Street and separate living quarters above. Lillian's VW bug sat in another Summerlin at Your Service spot. Straddling the remaining two spots was a black Porsche convertible parked at a jaunty angle, as if the driver simply couldn't bother parking straight, or taking only as much space as needed. The front vanity plate read XTREME. Violet climbed out of her car and tamped down irritation.

The man was *extremely* cocky, that was certain.

Of course, when she walked into her office, she was reminded why.

Dominick Burns was, as her Grammy would say, as fine as frog hair.

He leaned on the edge of her assistant's desk, his long legs stretched out in front of him. His dark brown hair was ridiculously sun-streaked and wind-tousled for December. His deep blue eyes were surrounded by the longest, darkest lashes imaginable. Ruggedly tanned and dressed in holey jeans, a gray Emory University sweatshirt and worn leather sneakers, he looked more like a carefree student than the thirty-something head of a multimillion-dollar company.

Judging from the way they were laughing, he and Lillian, a petite fortyish woman with a pink streak through her spiky black hair, were sharing a grand joke. They hadn't even heard the bell on the door that announced her arrival. For some reason, that annoyed Violet. She had the uncomfortable feeling they might be laughing about her.

"Hello, Mr. Burns." Despite her blasé response to Nan, her heart stuttered in her chest when he turned his smiling indigo eyes in Violet's direction.

"Vee, how many times have I told you to call me Dominick?"

"And how many times have I asked you not to call me Vee?"

He shrugged. "A couple hundred." Then he looked at Lillian. "In case you haven't noticed, your boss is a little uptight—"

"Here are your cigars," Violet interrupted, handing him the box. "Perhaps we can continue this in my office?"

Dominick grinned at Lillian. "I think I'm in trouble—and I like it."

Violet didn't respond, just walked toward her

office, mentally shaking her head. The man was a big kid.

He gamboled into her office and she reiterated silently the word *big*. He took up what little extra space the room had to offer outside of her desk, two chairs and row of file cabinets. "So you work on this level and have a condo above?"

"That's right. It's small, but it works for me."

"Nice location, near Piedmont Park."

"Another plus," she agreed, then gave him a wry smile. "And there's decent parking—as long as clients don't take up two spaces."

"I won't be here long," he said with a grin, sipping his coffee as he glanced around at the stark decor. He nodded to her desk, which was marred only by a neat stack of manila folders. "It's so *neat*. Do you actually work in here?"

"Yes."

She turned to set aside her bag and when she looked back, the folders were strewn across her desk in disarray. Dominick was looking at the ceiling and whistling like an innocent little boy.

"Nice," she said dryly.

He laughed. "Come on, Vee, loosen up."

"Mr. Burns," she said coolly, "I'm good at my job because I'm a detail-oriented person. Now, what can I do for you today?"

That elicited an eyebrow wag, which she ignored.

Then he sighed. "Okay, business it is." He reached into his jeans pocket and removed a crumpled piece of paper that looked as if it had barely made it through morning recess. "There's a company in Miami I'm considering buying. I need for you to do some research for me."

She read the words written on the paper. "Sun-piper Extreme Sports School?"

"Right."

"What kind of research?"

He shrugged. "Whatever you can find out—check the Internet, or make phone calls…anything."

"I don't know much about extreme sports," she admitted. "Perhaps I'm not the best person to do this…."

"I need someone I can trust, someone outside my office. As soon as word gets out that I'm making inquiries, the picture skews. People get greedy, and I don't know if I'm getting good advice from my advisors or if they're working for the other side."

When he was serious like this, his eyes warm and intuitive, she understood why the man was so successful. Beneath his carefree exterior beat the heart of a fierce competitor. He was…compelling. Violet averted her gaze and cleared her throat. "Okay. I'll get right on it."

He stood. "Good. If you find anything interesting, have it couriered to my house."

She stood and nodded. "Absolutely. Is that all, sir? Do you need any last-minute Christmas gifts?"

Dominick grinned and in a flash, he was back to being an overgrown frat boy. "You know me well. It's on the other side of that piece of paper."

She turned over the crumpled note and sure enough, on the back was a handwritten list. Not surprisingly, most of the names on the list were female.

He leaned forward over her desk, invading her space, his blue eyes twinkling with mischief. "What do *you* want for Christmas, Vee?"

Nan's comment about her needing something warm and cuddly flashed in her mind, but Violet pushed it away, especially since at the moment the turtleneck was feeling warm, if not cuddly. She drew back slightly and murmured, "World peace."

He laughed and shook his head. "If you were in charge, lady, I have a feeling you could make that happen. Thanks for the cigars." He pushed on wraparound sunglasses with reflective lenses, then walked out. "See you, Lillian," he called out as he strode out the front door.

Violet's new assistant was in her office before the bell on the front door stopped ringing. "What an interesting man."

Violet gave her a knowing smile. "I see you've fallen under Dominick's spell."

"You haven't?" Lillian asked, nodding to Violet's

hand, which had pulled out the collar of the turtle-neck and was fanning it open and closed to deliver some much-needed air.

Violet dropped her hand. "No," she said with more vehemence than she intended, then reached for the bundle of mail Lillian held. "I mean, he is a client, after all. I need his business more than I need his…er…"

Lillian arched an eyebrow, waiting.

Violet's cheeks warmed. "Were there any calls while I was out?"

The woman handed over a stack of pink slips. "If there's something I can take the lead on, let me know."

A proprietary feeling crowded Violet's chest. "I will," she murmured, while admitting she wasn't willing to entrust her clients to her new assistant yet. Maybe after the first of the year, when things slowed down, she could get to know Lillian better and begin delegating more to her desk. "Thanks for bringing in the mail. Do you mind taking Mr. Burns's coffee cup? And close the door as you leave."

"No problem," Lillian said with a smile, backing out.

Violet turned on her laptop, intending to start re-searching the company for Dominick. While she waited for the machine to boot up, she sifted through her mail, sorting things into neat little piles as she went. Trash, bill, bill, payment, junk, junk, junk—

Her hand stopped when she noticed a return address of Jacksonville, Florida, on a long white envelope. Covington Women's College, her alma mater? Probably a fund-raiser of some kind, she guessed. She slit open the top and pulled out a cover letter enclosing a pink polka-dotted envelope that tickled a memory chord. Intrigued, she scanned the letterhead—*Dr. Michelle Alexander.*

Violet frowned. Her former college instructor?

Dear Ms. Summerlin,

You were a student in my senior-level class titled Sexual Psyche at Covington Women's College. You may or may not recall that one of the optional assignments in the class was for each student to record her sexual fantasies and seal them in an envelope, to be mailed to the student in approximately ten years' time. Enclosed you will find the envelope that you submitted, which was carefully catalogued by a numbered code for the sake of anonymity and has remained sealed. It is my hope that the contents will prove to be emotionally constructive in whatever place and situation you find yourself ten years later. If you have any questions, concerns or feedback, do not hesitate to contact me.

With warm regards,
Dr. Michelle Alexander

Memories pelted her. The Sexual Psyche class had been called Sex for Beginners by all the students. She'd felt very naughty for taking it. She deliberately hadn't mentioned it to her grandparents and she'd sat on the back row—at first. But as Dr. Alexander lectured on the virtues of becoming a confident lover, Violet had gradually migrated toward the front of the class. She'd been a late bloomer in her teens, shy and self-conscious, her nose buried in books. Thanks to an absent mother and an old-fashioned grandmother, she'd never really had a proper sex talk. The class had been revolutionary for her, stirring up all kinds of… sensations and…urges. She vaguely recalled the assignment to write down her fantasies, remembered struggling to find the right words, but she couldn't recall what she'd written.

Violet looked back to her laptop, which was running a virus check. Then she pursed her mouth and tentatively picked up the pink envelope. There was only one way to find out.

2

VIOLET REMOVED two sheets of folded stationery from the small envelope, her heart thumping in anticipation at getting a glimpse into her own mind ten years ago. She had been so serious back then. The Sex for Beginners class had jarred her out of her comfort zone, if for only a few weeks.

She glanced at her closed office door, then unfolded the sheets and began to read.

Dear Violet,

I'm having a hard time with this assignment, writing down my sexual fantasies. I'm still getting used to the idea of what's even supposed to happen during sex. I've only done it a couple of times, and both times it was over before I even got my shirt off.

I have to say—if that's all there is to sex, I'm not impressed. It all seems rather…boring. Doing it in a bed, for instance—it seems like an invitation to go to sleep! Which is exactly what both guys did, by the way. Can't people have sex in other places besides the bedroom?

Or maybe it's just me. Maybe I'm not exciting enough to keep a man interested long enough to do it…well. I know that guys think I'm boring and uptight. I think so, too. Sometimes I feel like I'm trapped inside myself. I'm trying to get out, but I can't. I want to change, I just don't know how.

Dr. Alexander says she'll send us these letters in ten years. If you're reading this, Violet, I hope you're not boring anymore. I hope you've found someone who knows how to make sex exciting. I hope you've found a way out of yourself.

A rap on the door made Violet jump. She shoved the letter under a folder on her desk just as Lillian poked her head inside.

"Violet—" The woman stopped. "Are you okay?"

Violet nodded, sitting up straighter and running her hand over her flushed neck. "Yes, I'm…fine. What's up?"

Lillian grinned and held up a tin. "My weight if the sweets keep rolling in here. Want some fudge?"

"Not right now, thanks," Violet said, remembering she hadn't yet had lunch. "Who sent it?"

"Gail's Gourmet Candy."

"Oh, I'm sure it's good. I shop there for my clients. You can take it home if you like."

"Thank you, I will." Lillian started to leave.

"Lillian?"

"Yes?"

Violet swallowed, then lifted her chin. "Do you think I'm…boring?"

Lillian looked surprised and was quiet for a few seconds. "Violet, I think you're one of the most talented people I've ever met. You can do almost anything."

"But?"

Lillian moistened her lips. "But…you don't seem to make room in your life for fun."

Violet felt her defenses rise. "It's hard to have fun while running a business."

"I don't know. Dominick Burns seems to be having a ball," Lillian said with a little smile, then closed the door.

Violet chewed on her lip, considering the woman's words. She did too have fun—all kinds of fun, all the time.

Like the time she…

And sometimes when she…

Violet frowned hard. Fun was overrated. Fun led to…abandon. And recklessness.

And a loss of control.

Dominick Burns's handsome grin flashed into her head. *What do you want for Christmas, Vee?*

Now *there* was a man who'd probably had sex outside the bedroom.

Unbidden desire curled in her stomach and her breasts grew heavy. Dismayed at her reaction, Violet turned her mind to the task at hand—the research he'd asked her to do. Because for all his indiscriminate flirting, Dominick was more interested in her brain than her bod.

For the next couple of hours, she compiled everything she could get her hands on regarding Sunpiper Extreme Sports School—classes, instructors, press releases, videos, capital assets, endorsements, affiliations with sanctioned competitions, lawsuits past and present, as well as background on the two founders. At the school, one could enroll in classes to learn everything from rock climbing to dogsledding, either at the facility or at remote locations all over the world. The company had started small, but had grown steadily and seemed to be poised for either expansion or a new direction. She would keep digging, but on the surface Piedmont looked like a viable acquisition. In fact, Dominick wasn't the only suitor in the game—less than a month earlier, a company named Cambrian had publicly expressed interest in acquiring the sports school.

She was excited and flattered that Dominick had asked for her help on such an important matter. For all his tomfoolery, the man obviously trusted her, and it felt good to be appreciated for something more than picking up after a spoiled dog.

Violet sorted through the scattered printouts on her desk, wrote a note to Dominick on her company letterhead, informing him that she was still pursuing other avenues of research, and stuffed it all into an envelope. When her mind started creeping back to the letter she'd written in college and to the way Dominick's backside looked in those holey jeans, she gave herself a stern lecture.

The letter was nothing more than the naive ramblings of a sheltered coed in an all-girls school, whose teacher had made her feel daring for a short while. Sex had gotten better after college....

Some.

At least it wasn't over as quickly. But the journey from point A to point O was still a little...ho-hum. Or, at least it had been, the last time she checked.

Violet frowned. She hadn't had a serious date in months, she suddenly realized. She'd been so busy at work, and now with her parents back in town...

Not that she saw them that often, she thought with a pang.

They had an active social life, she reminded herself. Much more active than hers.

Unable to ignore her empty stomach any longer, Violet glanced at her watch and decided that if she left now, she could get ahead of rush-hour traffic, grab a bite at the food court in the Lenox Square mall and return Ms. Kingsbury's packages. Plus she could get a head start on Dominick's gift list. And the holiday atmosphere would help to put her in the spirit to celebrate Christmas with her parents.

She grabbed the stack of phone messages to return on the way. As she was leaving, she handed the bulging envelope to Lillian. "I'm taking off for the day. Could you please get this package ready for a courier, arrange for a pickup and have it delivered to Mr. Burns's home address?"

"Absolutely. Is there anything else I can do?"

Violet hesitated, then spied her cluttered desk through the open door to her office. "You can toss all the papers on my desk that aren't in a folder."

"Okay, great," Lillian said, brightening more than the situation warranted.

Violet set down her bag and fished out three of the phone messages. "And would you handle these clients, please? Call me if you have any questions."

"I will," Lillian promised, clearly pleased with the added responsibility.

Violet left, crossing her fingers that the woman didn't do anything that might jeopardize everything Violet had worked so hard to build.

DOMINICK FROWNED when he realized that the ice in his vodka tonic had melted. "You're slipping, old man," he muttered to himself, then poured the drink down the bar sink.

He'd been restless for weeks and in truth, he couldn't put his finger on the reason why, except for the fact that the holiday season always made him antsy. No longer having family left a gnawing feeling in his gut anytime of the year, but being alone at Christmas was the worst.

A knock sounded at the door. He looked up to see his longtime housekeeper, Sandy, standing there. "I'm heading home unless you need anything else."

"No, I'm fine," he said.

She angled her graying head. "Are you, Dominick? You've been moping around for months now."

He gave her a wry smile. Sandy had known him since he'd been a teenager driving his parents crazy with all his extreme sports activities, and she didn't miss a thing. "Don't mind me, I'm just bored."

"And lonely?"

He pursed his lips. "Maybe."

"You need to stop trying to kill yourself jumping out of airplanes and settle down. I've seen a dozen women come through here in the past few months. Aren't any of them marriage material?"

He walked over and put his arm around her shoulder. "I'm the one who isn't marriage material."

"You're not afraid to jump off a cliff into the ocean, but you're afraid to walk down the aisle?"

"Sandy, there are some things that are even too scary for *me* to attempt."

She made a rueful noise. "One of these days, son, you're going to meet someone who makes you feel more alive than any of those stunts you pull. When you do, promise me one thing?"

"What?"

She poked him in the arm. "That you'll jump. Good night."

"Good night," he said, planting a kiss on her cheek.

After Sandy left, Dominick reasoned that he'd been cooped up in his office too long, that he needed to plan a getaway and do something fun. The thought perked him up. He hadn't tried the new wingsuit that research and development had sent to him. After all, nothing said fun like jumping out of plane and riding the wind currents miles above the earth with the ground rushing toward you at breakneck speeds. The sensation was as good as sex.

Lately, even better than sex.

He considered calling Bethany, his current lover, but he was growing weary of her conversation—the woman was obsessed with reality shows. Call him old-fashioned, but he'd rather live life than watch it on a flat screen.

He thought about pouring a fresh drink, but couldn't work up the enthusiasm. He needed…something. A new challenge. Things were beginning to feel stale in his life. Maybe that's why the potential acquisition of Sunpiper intrigued him—it would give him something new to throw himself into.

When his doorbell rang he was glad for the diversion.

A courier looked him up and down. "Dominick Burns?"

"That's me," he said cheerfully, although he realized that one might not expect the owner of a home in this neighborhood to answer his door barefoot, wearing jeans and a retro Hang Ten T-shirt.

He signed for the package and tipped the guy. When he saw the return address, a smile curved his mouth. So Violet Summerlin had compiled information on Sunpiper already. The woman was a dynamo. He'd tried to steal her away as his personal assistant several times, but she'd turned him down flat. And he respected her for it. No one knew better than he did that the best job in the world was working for oneself.

Besides, if she was on his direct payroll, he couldn't flirt with her until her cheeks turned that adorable shade of pink.

As he opened the package, the image of Vee came into his head. Between the staid black-and-white uniform she insisted on wearing and that damn ponytail that was so tight the rubber band might blind someone if it snapped off and caught them in the eye, she was perhaps the most prim package he'd ever encountered. Still, he had eyes and the woman was classically beautiful. Her hair was thick and curly and she didn't miss being a redhead by much—a strawberry blonde he'd heard his secretary describe her as once, with the milky coloring to match. Despite her freckles, he doubted if the woman had ever spent a full day in the sun.

In fact, he thought, chuckling, there were probably parts of her that had yet to see the light of day.

But she had the most incredible blue-green eyes and full coral-colored lips. And he could see the generous curve of breast that she hid underneath her somber jackets. Violet Summerlin was stacked—she just didn't want anyone to know. He wondered idly if she had a boyfriend or if she spent all her time pleasing people like him.

Furthermore, he wondered if anyone had ever tried to please *her.* A vision of parting her knees to delve into those unexposed places made his cock twitch unexpectedly.

Dominick pulled his hand down his face and chastised himself for thinking such wicked things about such a sweet person, a person who wanted world peace for Christmas, for heaven's sake.

He decided to switch to coffee to peruse the information she'd sent, tossing an extra scoop of grounds into the filter for a caffeine kick. While he waited for the coffee to brew, he pulled the stack of papers out of the envelope. Violet's handwritten note to him was simple and to the point—she had arranged the research starting with high level, moving to more detailed.

More to come, the last line said, then she'd signed her initials.

He liked the way she communicated—quick and to the point. But her handwriting surprised him with its large letters and lots of swoops and curves. It seemed...romantic.

The thought conjured up another image of Violet, nude on pink satin sheets, her hair unbound and fanned around her head, her pale breasts high and full, with puffy pink nipples, her legs long and slender. When his cock hardened, Dominick scoffed at his reaction. He'd had a lot of women in his bed, all of them fit and tan and physical. Violet Summerlin was about as far from his type as he could imagine. She didn't smile easily, could never be described as bubbly or fun. As intriguing as it might be to try to bed her, she struck him as a lights-off-during-sex kind of girl.

He poured a cup of coffee, settled into a chair in the den and turned on a Hawks basketball game in the background. Over the next couple of hours he alternately read and checked the game score. Working through the material Vee had compiled, he mentally ticked off answers to some of his uppermost concerns. On the surface, Sunpiper looked like a good acquisition.

But things weren't always what they seemed.

When he turned the page, he frowned at a pink polka-dot envelope that looked incongruous next to the rest of the printed research. Had something been inserted in the package by mistake?

On the outside of the envelope were some kind of doodled numbers and letters…or a code?

He withdrew the pages and unfolded them. From the salutation, he first thought it was a letter to Violet and he started to refold it. Then he recognized the handwriting as hers—the same large letters, the same whorls and loops—and his curiosity intensified.

Noting the date, he soon realized that it was a letter that Violet had written to herself when she was in college. A couple of lines into it, though, his eyebrows flew up. Violet had recorded her sexual fantasies? As he read her words about her uninspiring sexual experiences, he shook his head. College-age boys weren't the most giving lovers.

But when he read the part where she questioned her own desirability, a pang of remorse barbed through him. These were the words of a lonely woman who felt overlooked and unloved. No wonder she downplayed her beauty—the more men ignored her, the more she probably wanted to be ignored. But in the letter she'd written, it was clear that she'd had hopes and dreams for her future that included exploring her sensuality.

I hope you've found someone who knows how to make sex exciting. I hope you've found a way out of yourself.

Dominick stood and walked back to the bar, the coffee forgotten as his need for a stiffer drink returned with a vengeance. His pulse pounded in his ears, sending adrenaline racing through his bloodstream. He'd been looking for a challenge and one had literally fallen into his lap.

He poured a vodka tonic and took a healthy gulp.

Quiet little Violet Summerlin with her tight ponytail secretly fantasized about exciting sex?

An energized smile lifted the corners of Dominick's mouth. This changed everything.

3

Five days until Christmas

WHEN VIOLET'S ALARM went off the next morning, it jarred her from a deep and disturbing dream starring Dominick Burns. The details were foggy, but it had something to do with being dangled from a high place…naked…with him promising to catch her. Her subconscious had managed to take her phobia of heights, as well as her phobia of being attracted to Dominick, and combine them in the most torturous way. Her body still pulsed with adrenaline and desire. She hit the off button on her clock and groaned.

That darn letter had unleashed all kinds of errant thoughts—and she was attaching them to Dominick simply because of his proximity and the work she was doing for him. Not because she was attracted to Dominick. She wasn't like all those women he dated; she was above the fray. They shared a professional relationship, which was way better than being one of his floozies.

A tremulous sigh escaped her heated body. Wasn't it?

Knowing she'd feel better after a shower, she pulled herself out of bed to face the day. Except today, the soapy sponge seemed to have fingers—long, tanned fingers that caressed her body in places where no man had ever touched her—her shoulder blades… behind her knees…the arch of her foot. She tried to push Dominick from her mind, but her body was pent up from the words that she'd written long ago and refused to let go of the image. Finally, following her previous advice to Nan, she turned the water full blast on cold. The icy sluice made her gasp, but it effectively drove all illicit thoughts from her mind.

She turned off the water and used a towel to briskly dry and warm her skin. Then she tuned into a radio station of holiday golden oldies to listen to as she got ready for work. "I'll be Home for Christmas" was her favorite Christmas song of all time. In her opinion, no one sang it like Doris Day, but any version would do. It never failed to make her feel all warm and tingly inside. This year the tune was especially poignant because her parents would be home for Christmas.

From now on, she'd direct all of her excess energy toward the magical holiday she would have with her family this year, not on Dominick Burns.

After Violet dressed, she double-checked the box

of Christmas decorations she was taking with her when she had lunch with her mother today—yards and yards of tinsel, old-fashioned bubble lights for the tree and new buildings for a miniature village she and her Grammy had enjoyed adding to each year. She'd wanted to put up the tree weeks ago in the den where it always stood and could be seen from the street, but her mother had suggested that they wait until Christmas Eve—a new family tradition. Violet had agreed, although she missed popping over to enjoy her Grammy's tree and bringing new orna-ments to hang on it every few days leading up to Christmas. She was taking over decorations a little at a time so there wouldn't be as much to transport Christmas Eve. On impulse, she added the gifts for her parents to the box. Maybe the gaily wrapped packages would persuade her mother to put up the tree early.

She idly wondered what Dominick Burns would do to celebrate the holidays. He'd never mentioned family and she'd never asked. Regardless, he didn't seem like the type who would want a Norman Rockwell Christmas.

What do you want for Christmas, Vee?

As Violet locked the door to her condo, she banished the memory of his mischievous blue eyes from her mind. Then she lugged the box of decora-tions, the gifts, her coat and her purse downstairs to the Summerlin at Your Service office while stifling a yawn. At this rate, she'd never make it through the day. One thing was certain, she couldn't afford to lose another precious night's sleep to foolish dreams stirred up by a silly letter she'd written in college. After unlocking the front door and turning the sign to Open, she started the coffeepot, then walked into her office, on a mission.

The sooner the letter met the shredder, the better.

But when she glanced at the lone neat stack of manila folders on her desk, panic blipped in her chest. She'd asked Lillian to discard the remnants of her printed research for Dominick—everything on the desk except for the folders. What if the woman had found the letter and read it?

Her cheeks burned. If that was the case, she wasn't sure she could face Lillian again. She flipped through the folders, but didn't find the pink envelope containing the letter.

The bell on the front door sounded, along with a happy humming noise, signaling Lillian's arrival. Violet walked out of her office and gave the woman a tentative smile. "Good morning."

"Good morning," Lillian returned, smiling wide as she hung up her coat and colorful scarf.

Violet bit into her lip, her nerves bundling tighter as her imagination spun out of control. She didn't know Lillian very well. What if the woman had read

her letter and gossiped about its contents? Violet
had worked so hard to cultivate a professional reputation in the community. That stupid letter could
ruin everything.

"I was just getting some coffee," Violet ventured.
"Would you like some?"

"Sounds good."

Violet poured two cups, then handed one to Lillian
and blew on her own. "Lillian," she said, trying to
sound casual, "I left a small pink envelope on my
desk. Did you happen to see it yesterday when you
were cleaning up?"

Lillian sipped her coffee. "No. Are you sure it
was there?"

"Yes. It had polka dots?" she said, hoping to jog
her assistant's memory.

"I don't remember seeing it. Did you check underneath the desk? Maybe it fell in the floor."

Why hadn't she thought of that? She hurried back
into her office and crouched down to search, but
didn't see it.

Lillian's face creased in concern. "I might have ac-
cidentally thrown it away with the other papers. I'm
so sorry if I did. Has the garbage been picked up yet?"

Violet nodded and pushed to her feet, feeling oddly
conflicted. She didn't really want the letter—heck,
she'd been planning to shred it. But somehow, not
having it made her feel as if something had slipped

through her fingers. "It's okay. I was the one who asked you to straighten up. Besides, I don't need it."

"Are you sure?"

"Absolutely," Violet said with a resolute nod.

The office phone rang and Lillian left to answer it. Violet dropped into the chair behind her desk and sighed, feeling restless for no identifiable reason.

Lillian was back in a few seconds, her face animated. "Dominick Burns is on the phone."

A hot flush climbed Violet's neck. She wasn't keen to talk to the man so soon after washing the imagined imprint of his hands off her body, but she couldn't think of a good reason to put him off. "Thank you," she murmured, then touched a button to connect the call.

"This is Violet."

"Vee, hey, it's Dominick."

His voice sounded sleepy around the edges, so she guessed he hadn't been awake for long. But when a creaking noise echoed in the background, she realized with a jolt that he was still in bed. Was he wearing boxers or briefs? Or did he sleep in the nude?

"Are you there?" he asked.

"Uh, yes…I'm here," she said, swallowing hard. "What can I do for you, Mr. Burns?"

"Thanks for the research on Sunpiper."

"You're welcome, sir. But I'd planned to do more."

"Good. Because I'm going to Miami to see what

I can find out locally, and I need some help. I was hoping you'd agree to go with me."

Her pulse rocketed. A business trip with Dominick? "I…I can't think…I mean, I *don't* think—"

"I'll double your hourly fees for the duration of the trip."

Her eyebrows rose, along with visions of making an extra mortgage payment. "Wh-when were you planning to go?"

"I'm flying down tomorrow, returning on the twenty-sixth."

"Oh, I couldn't go," Violet said, exhaling in near relief. "This is the busiest time of the year for my business."

"Can't your assistant take over?"

"No." Violet knew she'd spend the few days before Christmas traveling all over the city wrapping gifts for people who realized they didn't have time to do it themselves. "Besides, I'm spending Christmas Eve with my parents."

"Oh." He sounded disappointed—and a little surprised that she had other plans. "Well, what if I got you back Christmas Eve morning?"

"I…still don't think that would be possible, sir. I have…commitments. I'm sure you can find someone else to assist you."

"But I want *you,* Vee. You agreed to help me with this research."

"Whatever I could find on the Internet or over the phone," she reminded him.

"If money is the issue—"

"It isn't," she interrupted, looking for a way out, or at least a way to postpone the conversation. "Maybe after the first of the year…"

"That won't work for me," he said. "I'm leaving for Brazil in early January, and since another company is interested in buying Sunpiper, I need to move fast. If you're worried about the sleeping arrangements, we would, of course, have separate rooms."

Her midsection tightened at the mere mention of beds, proof of just how untenable it would be to travel with Dominick Burns when her mind insisted on spinning fantasies about him. "I'm afraid my answer is still no."

"Okay," he said with a sigh. "I'm heartbroken. We would've had a blast, Vee."

"Thanks for the invitation," she murmured. "Good-bye." She hung up the handset, tingling all over. *I'm heartbroken. We would've had a blast.*

Apparently he wasn't planning to spend the holidays with his family. He'd be in Miami, partying with half-naked women in the sun and surf. Violet knew he wouldn't have any trouble finding someone else to go in her place to "help" him. In fact, if the rumors were to be believed, Dominick didn't mind being helped by more than one woman at a time.

Lillian appeared at the door again. "Everything okay?"

"Fine," Violet snapped, reaching for her calendar and a diversion. Feeling contrite, she forced a calming note into her voice. "Did anything materialize from the calls you returned yesterday?"

"One didn't go anywhere, but the other two customers are supposed to stop by this afternoon to drop off gifts to be wrapped. I noticed all the paper and ribbon in the workroom," she said, gesturing to the room behind her desk. "I have the price lists and I used to wrap gifts at Macy's. I can take care of the packages and deliver them, too, if you want."

Violet jotted notes, then stood and shrugged into her coat, already calculating how she could make it back in time to greet the customers herself. "I have to make a few pickups and deliveries this morning, as well as go by Ms. Kingsbury's, and have lunch with my mother. But I should be back before two."

"Is there anything I can do while you're gone?" Lillian looked hopeful.

"No," Violet said abruptly, then realized she was letting the tossed letter and the call with Dominick make her cranky. Neither situation was Lillian's fault. She manufactured a smile as she swept through the door. "Just hold down the fort until I get back."

"What if I happen to find the pink envelope you lost?"

Violet whirled around and leveled her gaze at the woman. "Burn it."

4

JUGGLING HER COFFEE, her purse, the box of holiday decorations and the gifts, Violet unlocked her car door, her chest clicking with renewed annoyance at herself. She shouldn't have opened the letter to begin with—it was causing her to get even more out of sorts than she usually did when she thought about Dominick. At least now that the letter was on its way to a landfill, she'd be able to forget the silly words she'd written back when she had been under the delusion that sex played a major role in a person's life.

That might be true for other people. But since college, she'd come to the conclusion that she just wasn't a sexual person, not like Nan, who made flirting look easy. Anytime a man talked to Violet, her practical mind skipped ahead to the inevitable disaster the relationship would become and her tongue would tie in knots. She didn't stand a chance against the swarm of pretty, playful Southern girls that Atlanta had to offer up.

But she had her business, she reminded herself as

she stopped to pick up and deliver dry cleaning at four different locations, selected twenty-five perfect poinsettias for a corporate holiday party and picked up six needlepoint stockings customized with the names of a client's grandchildren.

Besides, she thought wryly while shopping for gourmet items on Ms. Kingsbury's grocery list, she had more luck with the four-legged male types anyway. On impulse, Violet picked up a bag of treats for Winslow. Maybe if the dog ate more, he wouldn't be so picky about where and when he did his business.

When she arrived at the gaily decorated brick home, the dog was waiting for her at the door with his leash in his mouth.

"He's been sitting there all morning," Ms. Kingsbury said. "I tried to take him out several times, but he wouldn't go."

Violet handed over the woman's credit card from her "returns" shopping trip and set the bag of groceries on a table. "I'll see what I can do. Is it okay if I give him a treat?"

"Whatever you like, dear. Sometimes I feel as if Winslow is more your dog than mine."

After clicking the leash onto his collar, Violet retrieved a doggie treat from her pocket and let the pop-eyed Pekingese gobble it out of her hand. "Are you going to be a good boy today?"

He barked enthusiastically. Maybe she should take

treats in her pocket the next time she went to a bar with Nan, Violet mused. On the short walk to the park, she called her friend to say goodbye before Nan left town.

"Nan Wellington."

Violet could hear the clicking of a keyboard in the background. Nan was a staff writer for the *Atlanta Journal-Constitution*. "Are you busy?"

"Just counting the hours until I leave for Aruba," Nan sang. "I wish you were going with me, but I know how much you're looking forward to having Christmas with your folks."

"Yes, I am."

"You sound kind of down."

"Don't mind me, I'm just in a funk."

"You're never in a funk. What's wrong?"

"Dominick Burns asked me to go with him to Miami over Christmas."

The clicking stopped. "Are you kidding me?"

"He needed my help, of course. Strictly business."

"Violet, *tell* me you said yes."

"I can't go, Nan. I'm swamped with clients, and I'm spending Christmas Eve with my folks, remember?"

"Oh, right. Well, can't you come back early?"

"He offered. But that doesn't help me take care of all the business I still have between now and then."

"How many times do I have to tell you that's what your new assistant is for!"

"I just don't feel comfortable letting someone else take over."

"Violet, I know you like to think that you have a special bond with your clients. But all they really want is to have things done for them, right?"

"Right," Violet admitted.

"So you wouldn't have hired this woman if she wasn't qualified. Let her help you."

"It's not that simple," Violet said. "I've been trying to delegate things to her, but because I'm not used to working with someone, there's already been a mishap."

"What kind of mishap?"

"I think she threw away a letter."

"So call the sender and have them resend it. Mistakes happen, sweetie."

"This was a personal letter. A handwritten letter."

"From whom?" Nan asked, her voice brimming with curiosity.

"From…me. It was a letter I wrote to myself when I was in college."

"Sounds cool. Did you find it in a yearbook or something?"

"No, the instructor sent it. The assignment was to write down your…thoughts. She promised to track us down and send the letter back to us ten years later."

"To see how much things have changed?" Nan asked.

"Or not," Violet murmured, realizing that for the

first time, she was conceding she still entertained some of the fantasies she'd written about.

"What class was it for?"

Violet hesitated, then wet her lips. "Sex for Beginners."

"Come again?"

"The class was called Sexual Psyche, but everyone referred to it as Sex for Beginners."

"So that's what goes on in those all-girls schools," Nan teased.

"It was just one class," Violet said, tingling with embarrassment.

"So what was in the letter? Your sexual experiences? Your fantasies?"

Violet didn't respond.

"Oh, my God. You wrote down your sexual fantasies! What were they?"

"Never mind," Violet said, exasperated. "It was a silly assignment."

"I think it's fascinating. In fact, it would make a great story for the paper."

"*No,* it wouldn't." Violet was in a near panic at the thought of being exposed.

Nan sighed. "Okay. So the letter went into the incinerator by mistake?"

"Looks that way."

"Did you at least get to read it?"

"Yes."

"And?"

"And…like I said, it was a silly assignment. I only brought it up as an example of why having an assistant isn't all it's cracked up to be."

"You need to give her a chance. You're never going to grow your company unless you hire people to work for you and delegate stuff to them."

"I know. And when things slow down after the first of the year…I'll think about it. I do hate the idea of passing up business. I could've earned a lot of extra money on this assignment."

Nan's wistful sigh breezed over the line. "But I guess it's just as well that you didn't take Dominick Burns up on his offer."

Violet frowned. "Why?"

"Well, he *is* a notorious playboy. He'd probably get you down to Miami and try to have his way with you."

Violet swallowed hard. "Do you think so?" she managed to say, her voice squeaking.

"Oh, sure. You'd probably have spent the entire time fighting off his advances."

"Yeah, that would've been…awful." Violet glanced down at Winslow, who had planted himself on the sidewalk, whining. "I guess I'd better go. Duty calls. Have a great time in Aruba."

"I will," Nan said. "Give your parents my best. I'll call you when I get back in town."

Violet said goodbye and disconnected the call,

then went through the steps of cajoling Winslow to do his thing. When he was finished, she carried him back to the house to save time. He practically purred in her arms.

"He did great," she said, handing him over to Patricia. "Merry Christmas, Ms. Kingsbury. Enjoy your time in Birmingham with your son and your grandchildren."

"Thank you, dear." Patricia Kingsbury ruffled Winslow's lion's mane. "I'm leaving in the morning, but the more I think about it, the more worried I am about taking Winslow with me. Between his reluctance to go potty and the fact that one of my grandsons has allergies…" She sighed. "Well, the truth is, Violet, I was hoping you'd be willing to take care of Winslow until I return."

Violet's eyes went wide. "Me?"

"You're staying in town for the holidays, aren't you?"

"Yes, but—"

"I'll pay you, of course. And I'd feel so much better if he were with you than in a kennel somewhere."

Violet didn't know whose eyes were more pleading, Patricia's or Winslow's. She wavered, reasoning that she could leave him at the office during the day and take him upstairs to her condo at night. And her folks probably wouldn't mind having him over Christmas Eve.

"Okay," she said, relenting. "But I can't take him with me now—my SUV is full of poinsettias and I still have a number of stops to make."

"I'll bring him over in the morning, on my way out of town," Patricia said quickly, as if she were afraid that Violet would change her mind. "I'll make sure you have his carrier and all his toys and things."

"See you then." Violet gave Winslow one last pat, then walked back to her car with hurried steps, checking her watch. She was looking forward to seeing her mother. They'd spent very little time together since her parents had returned to town. Violet had suggested meeting for lunch once a week to help them both get into a routine of seeing each other and sharing news. She was doing what she could to establish a mother-daughter relationship, and fortunately, her mother seemed amenable to her overtures.

When Violet pulled up to her grandparents' house, she was disappointed not to see a single light or decoration. She guessed that her parents had spent so many Christmases in foreign countries that they were out of the habit of decorating. She smiled as she pulled the box of decorations and the gifts from the front seat. She would do her best to get her parents into the holiday spirit. The trip up the well-worn steps to her childhood home never failed to warm her heart. While she had pined for her absent parents when she was little, her grandparents had made sure she experienced nothing but love and happiness in this house.

She pushed the doorbell with her elbow and leaned into the door frame to balance her awkward load. A few seconds later, her mother opened the door.

Violet smiled wide. "Hi, Mom."

Diane Summerlin was inserting an earring that matched her chic camel-colored ensemble. Violet had always envied her mother's casual elegance.

"Hello, Violet. Come in. What a nice surprise."

Violet's smile dimmed as she stepped over the threshold. "I thought we were supposed to have lunch today."

Her mother winced. "Were we? Oh, honey, I'm so sorry. I'm supposed to meet some old friends at the club."

Disappointment washed over her. "That's okay. We'll do it another time." She noticed that the furniture in the living room had been rearranged and the curtains were different. She'd assumed her parents would be making the home their own, but the changes were jarring.

Diane brightened. "I know. You could go with me."

But Violet knew a pity invitation when she saw one. "Thanks, but I have to get back to the office soon. Is Dad around?"

"He's playing golf."

"Oh." Violet tried to smile and patted the box she

held. "Maybe I'll just stick around here and get a head start on the decorations."

Her mother's smile faltered. "Um, Violet, about Christmas Eve…"

At the regretful note in her mother's voice, Violet's heart caught. "Yes?"

Diane touched her sophisticated blond bob. "Your father and I were invited to go on a cruise to Panama with the Tollesons."

Violet blinked. "Over Christmas?"

"The trip is all expenses paid. It would be a waste to let the tickets go unused, don't you agree?"

"Yes," she murmured, telling herself not to let her mother see how much their rebuff hurt.

"Your dad and I were thinking that we could all spend New Year's Day together, maybe go to the parade. Wouldn't that be just as good?" Diane's voice rang with false cheer. "You probably have friends with whom you want to spend Christmas anyway, don't you, honey?"

"Sure." Violet was proud of herself—she even managed a smile. "When do you leave?"

"Tomorrow." For the first time her mother looked contrite. "I was going to call you this afternoon."

Violet nodded. "Have a great time," she said with as much enthusiasm as she could muster. She set the gifts—the handmade coverlet and the set of carving tools—by the door, saddened that she wouldn't get to see them opened, but not sure that it mattered anymore. "Give Daddy my love."

Diane reached forward and kissed Violet on the cheek. "I will, honey. Merry Christmas."

"Merry Christmas, Mom." She looked down at the box of decorations she held, then turned to go, taking them with her. She kept her back straight and her tears at bay until she pulled out of the driveway and into traffic. And even then, she only allowed herself a few minutes to feel sorry for herself. She couldn't really blame Diane and Richard. The magical Christmas had always been her fantasy, not her parents'. They truly didn't understand what it meant to her for the three of them to spend Christmas Eve together. To them, it was no different than any other day of the year.

A profound loneliness enveloped her. Her grandparents had been her rock. Without them, her life and her heart seemed afloat. She knew that Nan was right—that since losing them, her workaholic tendencies had become more compulsive. She didn't need a shrink to tell her that she kept moving because she didn't want to acknowledge how empty her personal life was. But now it was staring her in the face. With Nan out of town, she didn't have anyone to spend Christmas with.

While Violet sat stalled in interstate traffic, her mind jumped among acquaintances, but there was no one with whom she was close enough that she'd feel comfortable inviting them to share the holiday. Although…Lillian had said she was staying in town for the holidays.

Which meant Lillian could probably work until Christmas Eve. Unbidden, the thought slid into Violet's mind.

She mentally reviewed the tasks left to do for various clients—a few last-minute gifts to buy, the pickup and delivery of a handful of tailored formalwear, but mostly, gifts to wrap. Gifts dropped off at the office and gifts at the homes of clients. Lots and lots of gift-wrapping.

But Lillian had stated that she had experience wrapping gifts. And the business was bonded against anything that might be damaged or broken while in their care.

Violet's mind started churning, rationalizing how she could arrange for Lillian to cover her commitments. Did she dare take Dominick Burns up on his offer?

He'd probably get you down to Miami and try to have his way with you.

A sheen of perspiration appeared on the rim of her lip. She was weary of being overlooked and underestimated, even by those who were supposed to be the closest to her. And she had to accept the blame for allowing it to happen. She was so quick to adopt the role of wallflower, of being seen, but not being heard. She was a spectator, staying on the sidelines and peeking like a voyeur into the exciting lives of others, instead of jumping in to her own. Even her chosen vocation of personal concierge meant always putting other people's needs first.

Frustration welled in her chest, crowding her lungs and pressing against her breastbone. A lifetime of wishing, hoping, wanting…things had to change.

Then suddenly something inside of her burst free and floated to the top. *Say yes to life,* she remembered Dr. Alexander saying in the Sex for Beginners class. Shaken by the revelation, Violet retrieved Dominick's cell phone number on her phone and pushed the button before she could change her mind. But with every ring, her pulse kicked higher and her confidence waned. She was fumbling for the disconnect button just as his voice came on the line.

"This is Dominick."

"M-Mr. Burns? It's Violet Summerlin. Um, I've been thinking…"

"Sounds dangerous," he said, his voice rich with amusement.

She blushed…and lost her nerve. She touched her forehead, trying to concoct a reason to have called. "I…might not be able to finish buying gifts for everyone on your list and get them to you before you leave town."

"I was planning to get you mailing addresses if

you wouldn't mind having them couriered to the people they need to go to."

"Oh. Of course I wouldn't mind."

"Good. Are you sure you won't reconsider and go with me to Miami?"

Her heart was beating so loudly she was sure he could hear it over the phone.

"Vee? Are you still there?"

"Yes, I'm here." Her palms were sweating. "Actually, my plans have changed. And if the offer is still open..." She gripped the phone harder and took a deep breath for courage. "I accept."

5

Four days until Christmas

THE NEXT MORNING, Dominick whistled happily as he packed his suitcase. After Violet had turned down his initial invitation to Miami for the manufactured holiday business trip, he'd nearly given up on the idea of getting her to himself—to seduce her and fulfill the fantasies she'd written about in her letter. Her about-face decision to go with him had electrified him. He'd barely slept last night from thinking about all the ways he would please her.

Admittedly, when he'd heard the tremulous note in her voice when she'd said, "I accept," he'd almost changed his mind. The woman was naive for her years and had most likely never been exposed to someone like him. He might scare her off and lose her as a business associate in the bargain.

But then he'd reminded himself that the trip was a win-win situation. He'd have help while he conducted research on Sunpiper, and Vee would be paid handsomely for her time. And if something else developed on the side, then they could indulge in a harmless holiday fling in a place where Vee didn't have to worry about being seen by anyone who might know her. His plan was to get the woman to let down her guard.

Or at least the collar of her ever-present turtleneck.

He picked up the pink polka-dotted envelope and his cock surged in anticipation. Violet hadn't mentioned the letter, so she obviously didn't suspect that it had somehow made its way into the envelope couriered to his house. Did she still yearn for the things she'd written about ten years ago? And would she be open to his seduction? If not, he wouldn't press her, of course. He'd never do anything to alarm her or drive her inhibitions deeper underground. But he hoped that she would allow him to be the one to show her how exciting sex could be.

He slid the envelope into the side pocket of his suitcase, simply because having it made him feel as if he were the keeper of a wonderful secret. It was better to give than to receive, and he planned to give Violet Summerlin a holiday vacation she'd never forget.

"Is that what you're wearing?" Lillian asked.

Violet looked down at her standard black suit and white turtleneck. "It's what I always wear."

Lillian pressed her lips together. "I know, and it's very professional. But you're going to Miami, and the dress code there is more informal."

"But it's all I have."

Lillian angled her head, then snapped her fingers. "We're about the same size, and I just picked up my dry cleaning."

Before Violet could protest, the woman was out the door, then returned in a couple of minutes with an armful of clothing contained in clear plastic bags. She hung the items on the coatrack, then flipped through them. "This blouse under your suit would be nice and cool."

Violet stared at the scrap of green fabric. "That's because there's nothing to it."

"It's a halter and it'll look great on you," Lillian insisted, pushing it into Violet's hands. "Here are two more blouses, and two dresses."

Violet bit her lip. The colors were brighter, the necklines were lower, and the hemlines were higher than anything she'd ever worn. "I couldn't," she said, shaking her head.

"Of course you can," Lillian said. "I insist. You might not need them, but if you do, at least you'll have them."

"Okay," Violet relented. "Thank you, Lillian. And thank you for agreeing to take care of things while I'm out of town." They had spent yesterday afternoon going over every detail of business that needed to be handled before Christmas.

Lillian smiled. "I'm glad you gave me another chance after throwing out that letter."

Violet lifted her hand in a dismissive wave. "It wasn't your fault. Forget about it. I have."

If only it were true. In truth, she couldn't get the words she'd written out of her head. *Sometimes I feel like I'm trapped in myself...I want to change, I just don't know how.*

So as nervous as she was about spending these next few days with Dominick, she sensed the experience would be eye-opening. Maybe simply being near the man would give her the courage to be more bold in her life choices going forward.

"Did you pack a bathing suit?" Lillian asked.

Violet squinted. "This is a business trip. Why would I need a bathing suit?"

"You'd be surprised how much business is discussed around pools and poolside bars, especially in Miami. You have one, don't you?"

Violet nodded.

"Then you'd better get it." Lillian checked her watch. "You still have time."

Resigned, Violet raced back upstairs to unlock her condo door.

"Don't forget sandals!" Lillian called.

Violet dashed into the bedroom, opening and

closing drawers until she found the bathing suit and cover-up that Nan had talked her into buying but she'd never had a chance to wear. She opened her closet door to fish out a pair of thong sandals that were practically new. When her gaze landed on a hanging lingerie bag, she hesitated. There was absolutely no rationale for taking a single piece of her little-used lingerie collection—gifts from Nan and purchases made at a lingerie party after one too many cosmopolitans.

On the other hand, as Lillian had pointed out, what would it hurt to take a few items, even if she didn't use them?

Violet wet her lips. But if she did need them, at least she'd have them.

She reached into the bag and pulled out a handful of silky things. After wrapping the cover-up around them, she hurried back downstairs to stuff everything into her suitcase.

When the front door bell chimed, her heart jumped to her throat. But when she looked up, she almost choked.

Patricia Kingsbury stood there smiling wide, holding Winslow in a carrier. "We're here!"

Violet swallowed a vile curse. She'd completely forgotten that she'd promised to keep Winslow over Christmas! Now what?

She conjured up a smile and introduced Lillian,

who was giving her sideways glances. Winslow began to whine, then bark in earnest until Ms. Kingsbury set the carrier on the floor and opened it to allow him to trot out. He went directly to Violet and rubbed her pants leg, leaving an astonishing amount of orange hair behind.

"Violet has a special way with my Winslow," Patricia gushed. "I think he's half in love with her."

"He's Pekingese, isn't he?" Lillian asked. "I've heard they can exhibit almost humanlike emotions."

"He has quite the personality," the woman agreed. "And when it comes to people, he certainly has his favorites." She clapped her hands. "Well, now that I know he's in good hands, I'm off. I'll be back on the twenty-seventh, Violet. You have my number if you need me, but I trust your judgment implicitly."

Violet nodded miserably while Winslow humped her leg. "Goodbye. Have a safe trip."

When the door closed behind Ms. Kingsbury, Violet held up her hands to Lillian. "Don't worry. I'm not going to ask you to take care of him."

"I wouldn't mind, except my landlady doesn't allow pets." Lillian crossed her arms. "I take it you agreed to this before you accepted Mr. Burns's invitation?"

Violet massaged her temple. "I can't believe I forgot."

Lillian looked down at the still-humping dog. "I can see why you would want to."

Violet sighed. "Winslow's really not that bad. He's just…temperamental."

"Sounds just like a man. What are you going to do?"

She shrugged. "I promised Ms. Kingsbury that I'd watch him. I'll have to tell Dominick that I can't go."

"Can you place the little fellow in a kennel?"

Violet grimaced. "Apparently, I'm the only one he'll go potty for."

Lillian laughed. "Like I said, you're the most talented person I've ever met."

"Thanks," she said wryly. "Besides, I wouldn't feel right about pawning him off on someone else, not when Ms. Kingsbury entrusted him to my care." She gently pulled the dog off her leg and reached for her phone, her heart heavy with disappointment. "I might as well try to catch Dominick before he gets here."

"Too late," Lillian said, nodding to the front door.

Violet looked out the window to see a black stretch limo sitting next to the curb. Her eyebrows rose at the unexpected luxury, and she nursed another pang of regret. The back door opened and Dominick stepped out, unfolding his long body. He looked casual but polished in dark jeans, black T-shirt and black shoes with a rugged sole. His wraparound sunglasses were sophisticated and cool. Violet's heart thudded wildly in her chest. She was almost glad now that she wasn't going with him. The man was simply too sexy for words. He removed his sunglasses, then walked up to the front door and opened it, causing the bell to chime.

Winslow went berserk, jumping up and down and barking in staccato spurts, as if stricken by Tourette's syndrome. Violet scooped him up to quiet him, murmuring soft words.

"Good morning," Dominick said tentatively, as if he detected something was wrong.

"Good morning," Lillian said brightly.

Violet stepped forward. "I'm sorry, Mr. Burns. I completely forgot that I promised a client I would keep her dog while she was out of town. I can't go to Miami with you after all."

He nodded to her suitcase. "But you're already packed."

"His owner just dropped him off. I was picking up the phone to call you."

Dominick pulled on his chin and walked toward her, squinting at Winslow. "That thing is a dog, you say?"

Violet nodded, her defenses rising on behalf of the homely little pet.

"Can't you kennel him?"

"No, sir. I gave my word I'd look after him."

He shrugged. "So bring him along."

Violet blinked. "It's very kind of you to offer, but I'm not sure if his carrier is the right size to allow me to take him onboard an aircraft as a carry-on bag."

A little smile curved his mouth. "I assumed you

knew that we'd be flying down in my private plane, Vee. There's plenty of room."

She wanted to thump herself on the forehead. Of course someone as wealthy as Dominick Burns didn't have to resort to anything as pedestrian as flying commercial. Still, she shook her head. "I don't think his owner would appreciate me taking him on a trip."

"Ms. Kingsbury wouldn't care," Lillian exclaimed, giving Violet a meaningful look. "I heard her say myself that she trusted your judgment implicitly. You'll still be looking after him, just in Miami instead of here. Besides, you'll be back before she returns."

Violet wavered. She wanted to go, but she'd never forgive herself if something happened to Winslow. "I'd have to be with him most of the time," she said to Dominick. "It might compromise the hours I can work for you."

"We'll work it out," Dominick said amiably. "If I remember correctly, the place where we're staying even has a doggie spa. And no offense, but he looks like he could use a beauty treatment or two."

She bit her lip. "Are you sure you don't mind?"

"Not at all. I like dogs." He reached forward to pet Winslow, but the Pekingese growled, then snapped at his hand.

"Winslow!" Violet admonished. "No!" She looked up at Dominick with a wince. "I'm sorry. I've never seen him snap at anyone. It must be all the excitement."

Dominick looked unconvinced. "Uh-huh. I'll get your bags, you bring the pooch."

She set down the dog and coaxed him into his carrier. Then she shouldered the bag holding Winslow's food and chew toys, picked up the carrier and headed toward the door that Dominick held open.

"Have fun," Lillian said. When Violet gave her a pointed look, the woman added, "And get a lot of business…transacted."

"Call me if you need anything," Violet said in her most professional voice. "I'll be available twenty-four-seven."

"Not planning to sleep while we're there, Vee?" Dominick murmured as she swept by.

She tripped, but he reached out to steady her before she and the dog both went down on the sidewalk.

"Easy," he said, his mouth close to her ear. "You won't be any good to me in a body cast."

The rough timbre of his voice skated across her nerve endings, stirring up all kinds of possibilities for the days ahead. When he opened the rear door to the limo, Violet hesitated, feeling oddly like Alice in Wonderland, contemplating whether to go down the rabbit hole.

"Are you having second thoughts?" Dominick asked.

She looked up, expecting to find a teasing expression on his handsome face. Instead, she was startled to see that his deep blue eyes were serious. "I want you to feel good about this, Vee," he said quietly. "But I promise to do my best to make sure you won't regret accepting my invitation."

She almost preferred the teasing Dominick to this more sober version who caused her midsection to warm and her breasts to tighten. Then her jaw loosened. Was that...*desire* reflected in his eyes? No. It had to be a trick of the winter light.

"Are you ready?" he murmured.

A shiver traveled up her spine. No more standing back and peeking into the exciting, sensual life she might have had if she'd been more daring.

"I'm ready," Violet said. Then she took a deep breath and climbed inside.

6

"I'VE NEVER BEEN on a private plane before," Violet said as they walked out onto the tarmac at the Fulton County Airport—known as Charlie Brown Airport to locals. Her heart was already racing at the prospect of hurtling through the sky in such a small aircraft.

Dominick grinned. "It's great. You get an entire can of soda."

She blushed under his gaze. He was enjoying the fact that he could introduce her to a new experience, and despite her fear of heights, she was determined to take it all in.

He handed their bags to a member of the ground crew who stood next to the open cargo compartment, then led Violet to the short set of steps leading up to the cabin. He reached for the dog carrier, but Winslow growled in opposition.

"It's not heavy," Violet assured him and proceeded to carry it up the steps, carefully balancing herself with the hand rail. Her nerves jangled like metal chimes as she stepped inside.

The plane had the smell equivalent to "new car," and indeed, looked as if it had just rolled off the showroom floor. The cabin was equipped with two rows of three seats facing each other, upholstered in gray leather. The spongy carpet was also deep charcoal-gray. A television was mounted over a counter that contained a sink. In the cabinetry underneath, a glass door revealed barware and snacks. A small refrigerator filled the remaining space. Racks on the sides of the cabinet held books and magazines. Every convenience for a comfortable trip had been provided, including a lavatory in the rear of the cabin.

"It's lovely," she murmured to Dominick. In truth, she was reeling at this glimpse into his wealthy lifestyle. She'd never seen his home, but could only wonder at the size.

He beamed. "I'm glad you like it."

The pilot emerged from the cockpit to greet them. The men were obviously well-acquainted and traded some flying-speak in terms of conditions and flight plans. When the pilot returned to the cockpit and Dominick turned to her, Violet felt awkward and jittery. "Is there someplace in particular we should sit?"

"Anywhere you like. You get a great view from the window seats."

"Thanks, but I prefer the aisle." She set her briefcase and Winslow's carrier on the floor and perched on the edge of the seat, gripping her knees.

His eyebrows arched. "Does flying make you nervous?"

"A little," she admitted, although not quite as nervous as Dominick made her feel with his casual confidence, his rugged good looks and his irresistible charm.

"I know just the thing to help you relax—love in an elevator."

She blinked. "Excuse me?"

His laugh rumbled out as he strolled to the bar. "It's a drink—Love in an Elevator. Ginger ale to settle your stomach." He winked. "Plus some gin and green Curacao liqueur to make it exciting."

"It's a little early in the day for me to drink," she protested.

"You're on vacation," he said, removing bottles and two glasses from the bar.

A little thrill curled up in her stomach. "I thought this was business," she reminded him.

"It's both." He mixed two drinks, then carried one back to her. "Humor me. I don't normally get to enjoy a drink when I fly."

"Why not?" she asked, taking the proffered glass containing a pale green liquid the color of the Caribbean water she'd seen in pictures.

Dominick lowered himself into the seat next to hers. "Because I'm usually either at the controls, or jumping out." He clinked his glass to hers. "Cheers."

She took a sip and when the fresh and sweet flavors burst over her tongue, she took another. "You have your pilot's license?"

He nodded.

She wasn't surprised, really, considering the fact that the man was an adrenaline junkie. "Why aren't you piloting today?"

Dominick shrugged. "I thought maybe we could… talk."

"I do need to review your gift list with you," she said, taking a deeper drink from her glass.

"Okay," he said, leaning into her, "we can do that."

From the carrier on the floor, Winslow lapsed into a fit of angry barking, pawing and pushing his snout against the mesh cutout in the door.

"What's with him?" Dominick asked.

"Er, I think it's you. He seems to be a little… jealous."

He frowned. "Jealous?"

"Pekingese are known to be possessive."

"Mr. Burns, we're ready for takeoff," the pilot announced over an intercom speaker.

"Where do you want me to put Winslow's carrier?" she asked.

Dominick set down his drink. "I'll take care of it." He picked up the carrier and set it on one of the seats opposite them, which triggered another torrent of barking. Dominick winced as he drew a seat belt around the carrier to secure it. "Is he going to be like this the entire trip?"

"I hope not," Violet said earnestly, then leaned forward and quieted the dog with a few comforting noises.

"You do seem to have a way with him," Dominick observed humorously, then raked his gaze over the length of her. "Would you like for me to take your jacket?"

She shook her head and realized that the alcohol was already making its way from her empty stomach into her bloodstream. Feeling self-conscious, she pulled the lapels of her jacket closed. "No, thanks, I'm fine."

But he was still looking her over. "You do realize that we're going someplace even warmer than Atlanta, yes?"

She squirmed beneath his gaze. "Yes."

"Did you at least bring a swimsuit?"

"Um, yes."

He smiled and nodded, apparently satisfied that she wasn't a complete stick in the mud. She silently thanked Lillian for insisting that she pack casual clothes, and took another drink from her glass.

"Buckle up," Dominick said, reclaiming his own seat. "We're expecting to hit some turbulence and you look like you bruise pretty easily."

She flushed under his teasing glance, but the alcohol was loosening her tongue. "I might be able to withstand more than you think, Dominick." She realized, with a little tingle, that for the first time she'd called him by his name to his face.

Something primitive sparked in his eyes. It was the same look she thought she'd imagined before they climbed into the limo. "Guess I'd better buckle up, too, then," he said, his voice low and sexy. "Something tells me this could be a bumpy ride."

It was.

Despite the relatively nice weather on the ground, once the plane reached cruising altitude, they encountered wind currents, sending the small aircraft bouncing along, jarring its inhabitants with enough force that Violet finished her drink quickly, lest it wind up all over her white turtleneck.

"I'm sorry," Dominick said over the forgotten gift list they were supposed to be discussing. Their heads were close, their shoulders practically touching.

She looked up, captivated by his blue-eyed gaze. "For what?"

He nodded to her white-knuckled grip on the armrest. "For the rough ride. Are you okay?"

Violet nodded. In truth, she was scared half to death. Every dip made her think how the very act of flying in an airplane was counterintuitive to human nature. When one was being tossed around in the sky, all the scientific and engineering advances in aeronautics didn't count for much. The bottom line was that they were literally hanging in the sky with no wires and no safety net.

What Dominick couldn't know, however, was that the adrenaline rushing through her body, sped along by the alcohol, had triggered a low hum of excitement deep inside her. And with every swoop and lunge of the plane, the vibration became more intense, triggering erotic firestorms all over her body. Her heart pounded, and her hairline was moist. Her breasts felt heavy and, scandalously, beneath her standard uniform pants, her underwear was wet with her own sensual lubrication. When she shifted in her seat, Dominick covered her hand with his.

"It'll be okay, I promise."

Violet stared at his hand, the long tanned fingers that she'd fantasized about touching her in places no other man had. Her nipples tightened to hard little buds as a flush enveloped her body. Her reaction to the danger, to his slightest touch, was beyond embarrassing. Dominick would laugh at her if he knew her subversive triggers.

"I need to go to the restroom," she said breathlessly, then pulled her hand from beneath his and fumbled with her seat belt.

"Let me help," he said, then reached across her in seemingly slow motion to release the belt's clasp.

When his hand brushed over her lap, Violet bit back a groan. Her body was honed to a fever pitch.

As soon as the strap fell slack, she stood and weaved her way toward the lavatory.

"Careful," Dominick called behind her.

Once she made it to the door, Violet opened it and slipped inside the small cubicle. A light came on automatically when she closed the door. The lavatory looked much like the bathroom of a commercial plane, with a commode, a tiny sink and a mirror. Violet steadied herself against the sink and stared in the mirror. Her cheeks were pink and her eyes were dilated. Her lips were parted because she couldn't seem to drag in enough air through her nose to supply her lungs. A strand of hair had escaped her ponytail. She looked…wanton.

When the plane dipped again, she gasped and braced herself. Here the drone of the plane engine was louder, the vibration more pronounced. Her heart galloped in her chest, and her sex felt heavy with need. How was she going to finish this plane ride without falling apart? Her state of arousal had her reading sexual undertones into Dominick's slightest movement. She was projecting her fantasies onto him. And at this rate, it wouldn't take much to send her over the edge.

Violet moistened her lips and glanced at the closed door. In fact, all she needed was a few minutes of privacy to relieve the tension….

Even as her hand slid inside the waistband of her

pants and the elastic of her panties, some part of her was mortified by her behavior. But, she reasoned, it was the quickest solution to her immediate problem. No one would ever know. When her fingers found the center of her desire, she sighed, massaging the button in small circles to coax the burgeoning orgasm from deep within her. It had been so long, and these last couple of days thinking of Dominick…being close to him…

The plane lurched, and her muscles contracted, sending the orgasm exploding through her body. Violet pressed her lips together to stifle her moans, and held onto the sink when her knees buckled from the sheer intensity of her release.

DOMINICK STOOD with his hand raised to knock on the bathroom door to ask Violet if she was okay. When he heard the moans inside, he winced and pressed his ear closer, dismayed that the plane ride he'd hoped would be fun had instead made the woman sick.

Then he frowned. The sounds coming from the other side of the door weren't the noises of someone in pain. In fact, if he didn't know better…

It almost sounded like…

Dominick's eyes widened in realization. Violet was getting herself off?

His cock surged as his mind reeled. But it made sense, he concluded. The woman hinted in her letter that danger and excitement turned her on. So the rough plane ride was…foreplay?

He pulled his hand down his face in wonder, but before he could fully digest the revelation about little Violet, the door opened. He stumbled backward, but caught himself.

She looked up in surprise, her full lips parted. Her cheeks were flushed and her eyes were slightly glazed. Knowing what she had been doing sent lust coursing through his body even as he tried to act innocent. "Are you okay?" he stammered.

"Yes," she murmured. "I'm…feeling much better."

Tension vibrated between them. His hands itched to touch her, but he didn't want to scare her off. He'd have to bide his time with this woman. Something told him it would be well worth the wait.

"Good," he said finally, then nodded to their seats. "We'd better buckle in."

He followed her back, although Dominick wasn't sure how he was going to sit with the raging hard-on her performance had inspired.

As he settled awkwardly in his seat, he released a long breath and glanced at Violet's profile. She tucked an errant strand of hair back into her ponytail and pulled her jacket more securely over her breasts. Back to prim and proper. The woman packed a powerful punch and didn't even realize it.

Dominick swallowed hard and shifted to ease the

discomfort in his jeans. He wanted this woman underneath him, in his bed, crying out in pleasure. His hunger for her had suddenly escalated from a mere challenge to a pulsing need. He couldn't wait to get Violet on the ground—and then sweep her off her feet.

7

BY THE TIME THE PLANE landed in Miami, Violet had regained her composure, but guilt plagued her. From the wary way that Dominick was treating her, he apparently thought she'd gotten ill in the bathroom, versus having gotten *off*. And she wasn't about to clear up the misunderstanding.

She'd learned something new about herself and it had left her shaken. But now that she'd hit the release valve, she should be fine, as long as she kept a lid on the excitement level.

Not an easy task when Dominick was in the vicinity. At the airport, he rented a Mercedes convertible, and they drove to South Beach with the top down. The landscape looked like a Technicolor postcard with palm trees spearing a turquoise sky and the sun casting a pink glow over everything in its path. Violet had never seen so much skin in her life. String bikinis and thongs abounded, with brown, glistening bodies extending into the horizon. Playing loud music and in-line skating appeared to be the prevailing outdoor activities. The atmosphere fairly pulsed with a sexual vibe. Violet shifted in the passenger seat as perspiration trickled down her back.

"Aren't you hot in that jacket?" Dominick asked with a grin.

"It's not too bad," she replied, taking another drink from the bottle of water she held. In truth, she was on the verge of melting.

Dominick, on the other hand, was sprawled in the driver's seat looking cool and collected and impossibly sexy.

She turned to check on Winslow in the backseat. He was scratching at the door of his carrier, obviously antsy at being cooped up for so long. She reached back to soothe him, touching her fingers to the mesh for him to lick.

"How much longer to the hotel?" she asked.

"Just a few more minutes to South Beach, then we can all stretch our legs."

"Are we staying near the Sunpiper Sports School?"

"Everything in Miami is relatively close. The city is densely populated, but not very big."

"Do you have specific plans for finding out more about the school?"

"Actually, I thought we'd go by there this afternoon, if that works for you."

"Of course. I printed out more research last night and brought a mini-laptop for note-taking."

He gave a little laugh and rolled to a stop at a light. Unexpectedly, he reached over and smoothed a loose hank of hair behind her ear. "Okay. But let's get to the hotel and eat lunch first. How does that sound?"

Violet inhaled sharply at his touch. From the backseat, Winslow barked angrily.

Dominick frowned and pulled his hand away. Violet wasn't sure whether she should be relieved or irritated at the interruption. Nan's words about Dominick trying to seduce her while they were in Miami reverberated in her ears. Would he?

And would she let him?

Her pulse was still clicking away when they pulled in to the valet parking area of the Catalina Hotel. She picked up Winslow's carrier and followed Dominick inside, feeling like a peasant ogling royalty. The art deco hotel was a five-star establishment with all the trimmings—lush landscaping, palatial common areas and white-suited staff. Violet spotted a movie star and a pop singer in the lobby, and tried not to stare. Dominick seemed to take it all in stride, which only made her feel more backward as he checked them in and led her toward the glass elevator. She was woefully overdressed and perspiring profusely. She kept pulling her turtleneck collar away from her sticky neck, trying to let some air in. And she wasn't looking forward to the ride up in a glass box.

She stepped on and plastered herself against the opposite wall. "What floor are we on?"

"We have a penthouse suite," Dominick said.

The elevator doors closed and they began to climb, but her fear of heights gave way to a greater fear. "Y-you said we would have separate rooms."

"Separate rooms," he confirmed, "but connected. So that I can get to you if…I need you."

From the carrier on the floor, Winslow growled menacingly.

The warning bell in Violet's head sounded in time with the elevator chime. The doors slid open to hushed opulence. When she alighted, the scent of ylang-ylang tickled her nostrils. Zen-like music played from hidden speakers.

She followed Dominick down the hallway, where a bellman waited with their luggage outside a double door. The uniformed man greeted them, then used his key to open the door and swept his arm for Violet to precede him.

The room was larger than her condo—and exponentially more grand. The entryway featured lush carpet, but at the bottom of a short set of steps, sand-colored floor tile with just a hint of pink stretched in all directions. A kitchenette and bar sat to the immediate left. Straight ahead, a wall of windows was the backdrop for a spacious sitting area. The furniture was pale overstuffed leather, cool and inviting. Sumptuous area rugs created islands of tranquility. A balcony off the living room offered panoramic views of the beach below and the Atlantic beyond.

"It's…wow," she murmured, at a loss for words.

Dominick laughed and she blushed, reproaching herself for her uncouth response. "I mean, it's lovely, Mr. Burns."

He frowned. "I thought we'd made it to a first-name basis."

Her face warmed. "Dominick."

He smiled. "I'm glad you like the accommodations. Traveling first class is one of the perks of the job." He turned to the bellman. "The black bag goes in the room on the right, the blue bag in the room on the left."

He walked over and opened the sliding glass door leading to the balcony, then stepped out. He gestured to her and she made her way gingerly to the doorway. She took a tentative step outside, swayed, then reached back to cling to the door frame for support. The balcony jutted out from the building like a long narrow box. The railing was frosted glass panels with lots of daylight in between. If the architect had intended for the occupants to feel as if they were dangling high above the earth straddling a beam, the design was a raging success.

"What a view," he said, leaning against the rail.

"I'll take your word for it," she murmured, then

stepped back inside and put her hand over her racing heart.

Dominick followed her and closed the door. "Too high for you?"

"And too small and too…open."

Inside the carrier, Winslow barked and pawed at the mesh window, demanding attention.

"Is it okay if I let him out?" she asked Dominick.

"Sure. I assume he's housebroken?"

"Oh, yes. In fact, I probably need to walk him."

He gave the porter a tip then glanced at his watch. "How about we take twenty minutes to freshen up, then we'll let Mr. Squatty Face have a walk and we can get a bite to eat?"

"His name is Winslow," she chided with a laugh. When she opened the door to the carrier, the dog practically leapt into her arms, wriggling and licking her face.

"Can't fault his taste," Dominick remarked, turning toward the door to his room. "Let me know if you need anything, Vee."

Violet carried Winslow to the door of the room where the bellman had taken her suitcase and tried not to think about the fact that there were only fifteen feet between the doors of their bedrooms. Five long strides. She gave herself a mental shake, pushed open the door and gasped.

The king-size bed sat in the corner at an angle,

facing the same view as the living area. The furnishings were luxurious, but understated. The thought flitted through her mind that it was the kind of bed that one shared, big enough for two. She peeled off her suit jacket and draped it over a chair, then stepped out of her loafers and socks and sank her feet into the deep pile of the rugs scattered over the oversized floor tile. The bathroom boasted a jet tub and enormous, fluffy towels, spa robes and luxury toiletries. She ran a hand over the sleek countertop and wondered if her parents had enjoyed these kinds of accommodations when they traveled. Probably, since her father had often worked for high-level government officials.

No wonder they hadn't wanted to come home, she mused.

Winslow followed her around, his toenails clicking on the tile floor. She crouched down to pet him, feeling a rush of affection for the homely little dog. She knew what it felt like to be abandoned at Christmas. From the bag that Patricia had packed, Violet withdrew his bowl and a resealable bag of dry food. She put a half cup of the food into the bowl so he could eat while she checked her phone for messages.

The fact that there weren't any left her with mixed feelings. She'd hoped her parents had left a message about the gifts she'd left or that they'd arrived in

Panama safely, or something to that effect. And she expected at least one phone call from Lillian about… something. She decided to check in, just in case. While she punched in the number, she unzipped her suitcase.

"Summerlin at Your Service, this is Lillian."

"Lillian, it's Violet."

"Hi. How was the trip?"

"A little bumpy," Violet admitted, pulling clothes out of her suitcase and hanging them in the closet on the padded hangers provided. "But we're here. I was just calling to see if everything is okay at the office."

"Everything's fine," Lillian said cheerfully. "I'm up to my elbows in gift wrap and ribbon, and later I'm going on a delivery run."

"So…no problems? Or…questions?"

"No, none."

Violet frowned. "Okay, well, in the next couple of days I'll be overnighting to you the last few gifts on Mr. Burns's Christmas list, and I'll need for you to hand-deliver them."

"Sure. No problem."

Violet worked her mouth. "My phone is on, so call me if anything comes up."

"I will," Lillian promised. "But don't worry. Things are under control."

"Thanks, Lillian. That's…good to know," Violet murmured, then said goodbye. But when she hung up, she conceded feeling a bit irked that her business could run so smoothly without her.

A quick check of her watch told her she had scant minutes to freshen up. She left the rest of the unpacking until later, then stared at her reflection in the mirror and sighed. She looked flushed and wilted. She removed her turtleneck and washed her face, then applied powder makeup to even out her freckles. She repaired her ponytail, trying to tame the extra curl that the humidity had brought out in her hair. When she picked up the turtleneck, though, she bit her lip. She would look ridiculous if she put it back on.

With trepidation, she fished out the green halter top that Lillian had pressed upon her. If she wore it, she'd have to forgo a bra. Dubious, she removed her bra and contorted to fit herself into the halter. It fit, albeit snugly, and she conceded that despite the yards of white skin showing, the top looked more appropriate to the climate than anything she'd brought with her. She pulled on the black suit jacket and pursed her mouth. She'd never shown so much cleavage in her life, but when in Rome…

Winslow whined and when she looked down, he was holding his leash in his mouth. "Okay, I'm hurrying." She pushed her feet into the sandals she'd brought, grabbed her purse and went to the bedroom door, wondering if or how Dominick would react to her new look. She hesitated. Was she trying too hard?

Winslow barked his impatience, so she took a deep breath and opened the door.

Dominick was waiting by the window, taking in the view. "How does seafood sound for lunch?" he asked, turning. When he saw her, he stopped and his eyes widened. "Vee…you look…wow," he said, mimicking her earlier response to the room. "That's better than the turtleneck."

She warmed under his gaze as he walked closer to her. "Thank you," she said primly. "And seafood for lunch sounds great—after I walk Winslow."

"We'll walk the pooch on the way," Dominick said distantly, although he didn't even glance at the dog at their feet.

She picked up Winslow, who bared his teeth at Dominick, then they all descended to the lobby. The concierge directed Violet to a place where she could walk Winslow and Dominick tagged along. She hoped desperately that the dog would go without his normal coaching, but after a few minutes of leading him up and down the shaded, grassy strip, it became apparent that he needed a nudge. So, swallowing her pride, Violet knelt and made little cooing noises in his ear. "You're such a good boy, Winslow, yes, you are. And you're so handsome, yes, you are, you good little doggie."

Winslow almost smiled, then obliged her with a squat. She turned her head to find Dominick staring, eyebrows raised. "You have to compliment the dog into taking a dump?"

She gave him a wry smile. "It's part of the job."

"You need to increase your fees," Dominick said.

She removed a plastic bag and disposable scoop from her purse to clean up after Winslow, then tossed it all in the nearest trash. "We're ready," she announced with a smile.

He looked down at Winslow. "And I thought I was demanding," he said to the dog. Winslow growled, then barked as if he were much bigger than his fluffy twelve inches.

Winslow continued to "guard" her, walking between her and Dominick as they strolled to a beach-side café for lunch. Violet had to scold the dog twice for snapping at Dominick. As they took their seats and she attached his leash to the leg of their table, it was clear there was no love lost between the two "men."

"Does he ever take a nap?" Dominick asked sourly, "or are we going to have to take him everywhere?"

"He'll be fine in my room for the afternoon," Violet said. "We'll have plenty of time to visit Sunpiper. And I still need to shop for some things on your gift list." She pulled the paper from her purse. "I left the other gifts with Lillian to be delivered. But there's still Heather, Mia, Sandy and Bethany. I need to get them soon to have them delivered to Atlanta for Christmas. Do you have any special requests?"

Dominick shifted in his seat. "Uh, the gift for Bethany should probably be some kind of jewelry."

A tiny barb of jealousy struck her chest. "Okay. A bracelet, perhaps? Earrings?"

"We'll talk about business later," he said, dismissing the list with a wave.

Violet nodded and stowed the paper, wondering if Dominick was thinking of something more serious for Bethany, like a ring. She idly wondered what Bethany thought of her boyfriend spending Christmas in Miami with another woman.

Not that she posed any kind of threat, Violet reminded herself. Nan had been wrong in her prediction. Because while Dominick had been friendly and even complimentary, so far he'd shown no inclination whatsoever that he intended to "have his way" with her.

Violet wiped at her heated brow, then picked up her water glass for a long drink, glancing beneath her lashes at his handsome profile.

Darn it.

8

THE WAITRESS CAME and took their order. Because of the heat, Violet wasn't very hungry, but since the only thing she'd had in her stomach today was the drink on the plane and some water, she ordered a shrimp cocktail and Dominick ordered a fish sandwich. They made small talk while they waited for the food. Violet felt awkward and stiff next to Dominick's relaxed posture. He was at ease with the casual lifestyle of Miami and it suited him. She, on the other hand, felt as if she were visiting another planet.

The people in Miami were proud of their bodies and their sexuality. Everyone flirted and touched and laughed and danced. Alcohol flowed like the sea itself, and public displays of affection were commonplace. People moved in pairs or in groups and everyone seemed open to just about any game that erupted spontaneously, from doing the limbo to tucking an orange under their chin and passing it down the line, rubbing bodies indiscriminately. Everyone seemed to be in party mode, whooping it up before Christmas. Garland hung incongruously from palm trees, and many sunbathers wore Santa hats.

Winslow whined for food from beneath the table but Violet shushed him with water poured into a plastic cup for him to lap.

When Dominick had finished with his sandwich, he folded his hands behind his head and stretched out his long legs. "What great weather, eh?"

She nodded, pulling a finger around the collar of her suit jacket. Dressed in the black suit, the sun's rays were brutal.

"I'm glad you came, Vee."

His offhand comment sent her pulse pounding— this man could so easily affect her. She swallowed and tried to match his breezy tone. "Me, too."

"I hope your folks weren't upset that you changed your mind about spending Christmas with them."

She wished she had her sunglasses to hide the sudden moisture pooling in her eyes, but she managed to look away and get a grip on her emotions. "No, they weren't upset."

"What do your parents do?"

"My mother is a teacher, my father is a translator. They spend most of their time outside the States."

"Sounds like an exciting way to spend your childhood."

"I mostly stayed with my grandparents in Atlanta," she said, playing with the napkin in her lap.

"Ah, so they'll miss having you there at Christmas."

"My grandparents passed on earlier this year," she murmured. "Only a couple of months apart."

"I'm sorry," he said, his tone low and warm.

"They lived a full life," she said, mimicking the words that people had told her at the time to make her feel better.

"Still, you must miss them," he said.

Her heart squeezed and she nodded. "Do you have a big family?"

He shook his head. "No. I'm an only child, and my parents have been gone for some time now."

It was a different side of Dominick. She had wrongly assumed from the man's happy-go-lucky demeanor that his life was carefree. "I'm sorry," she murmured, and reached for his hand before she caught herself and pulled back. "What do you normally do for Christmas?" she asked to cover her gaffe.

He shrugged. "Travel. Jump out of planes."

She smiled. "Or buy companies?"

"Maybe this year," he agreed, and the boyish hopefulness in his eyes caught at her heart. Warning flags waved in her mind. Discovering these tender things about Dominick wasn't a good thing. Harboring a crush on a certified playboy was safe because she knew better than to take him seriously. But when he let down his guard, she was tempted to think that he was more than the horny daredevil the press made him out to be.

The waitress returned with a drink, which she set in front of Dominick. "Sex on the Beach," she said, then pointed. "From the blonde over there."

Unable to resist, Violet turned to look at the stunning woman in a leopard-print bikini who gave Dominick a little wave. A flush of embarrassment climbed Violet's neck—the woman had obviously concluded that she and Dominick were too mismatched to be a couple. She quickly turned back around and pulled the lapels of her jacket closed, watching Dominick's reaction.

He picked up the drink and gave Violet a little smile. "Excuse me a moment."

He unfolded his long, muscular body and walked over to the blonde. Violet couldn't bear to watch, so she ruffled Winslow's ears and fed him pieces of shrimp from her plate, her face stinging. She supposed this kind of thing happened to Dominick all the time, beautiful women throwing themselves at him. It put the crush she had on him in perspective. She was pathetic.

He was back in a couple of minutes, without the drink, which he must have drained. "Ready to go?" he asked.

She nodded and untied Winslow's leash while Dominick left money on the table, along with the check. She shouldered her purse and left, walking slightly in front of him and fussing with the dog to hide the fact that her face was still burning. He'd probably made plans to meet the woman later.

Neither one of them mentioned the incident as they walked back. Anytime Dominick made the mistake of moving too close to Violet, Winslow let him know. When they reached the hotel, the dog latched onto Dominick's jeans leg with his razor teeth.

"Ow!" Dominick yelped.

"Sorry," she said, crouching to disengage the two. "Did he break the skin?"

"I don't think so," Dominick mumbled, rubbing at his ankle.

"He's probably still out of sorts from all the travel," she said. "Are we going to visit the sports school now?"

"If we can shake rabid Toto for a few hours."

"Let me get him settled in my room," she said.

"I'll get the car," he said irritably.

Violet smothered a smile as she carried Winslow onto the elevator. "You're a bad boy," she whispered.

The dog sighed against her neck. She petted him to keep her mind off the fact that she was racing in a glass box high above the ground. One of these days, she hoped to conquer her fear of heights.

In the room, she set Winslow down and put out water and a tiny bit of food. After scattering his chew toys around, she turned on the television and tuned it to *Animal Planet,* satisfied when the barking dogs on the show captured Winslow's attention. While he was diverted, she grabbed her laptop bag and purse, and let herself out, closing the bedroom door behind her. She took the service elevator down to the lobby— the ride wasn't as elegant, but it was safely enclosed.

Dominick was waiting for her in the car, sitting in the driver's seat, tapping his hand on the steering wheel in time to the song playing on the stereo. She took advantage of the moment to study him, and she saw what every other female saw—everything about the man screamed sex, from his wild, shaggy hair to his lean, muscular body. It wasn't a stretch to picture him doing all the extreme sports he was known to pursue. He exuded danger. Her midsection clutched with desire.

He saw her and waved. "Vee! Hey, I was getting worried about you."

She smiled, striding toward the car. "Sorry. I took the time to grab my laptop. Is someone at the school expecting us at a certain time?"

"No. In fact, no one there knows we're coming."

"Oh." She blinked. "Then how are we supposed to find out what you need to know?"

"I have a plan," he said, then smiled. "You'll see."

Something in the tone of his voice made her suspicious, but she held her tongue. She was, after all, here to work for him.

The streets were clogged with cars and pedestrians that streamed in between vehicles. The half-naked bodies and shouts of laughter pushed her pulse higher, and the overhead sun was merciless. Violet squirmed and edged open her jacket to catch any breeze that might be moving. She was roasting like a Christmas turkey.

"I can put up the top if you're too warm," he offered.

"That's okay," she said, knowing that she was being a prude. She leaned forward and shrugged out of her jacket, hoping that her expanse of white skin didn't cause an eclipse. When she settled back in the seat, she felt his gaze on the snug green halter top that cradled her breasts and dipped low enough to expose a deep valley of cleavage. Her breasts had always been the bane of her existence. Men seemed to be attracted to them, but the few guys she'd been with hadn't known what to do with them.

She turned her head to find Dominick looking at her, although she couldn't see his eyes behind the dark glasses he wore.

Then a sexy grin curved his mouth. "So that's what you've been hiding under those suits of yours."

His comment flustered her—she felt caught between pleasure and modesty. To her horror, her nipples hardened, and without a bra, it was noticeable to anyone who looked. And Dominick was looking, which only made them harder. She sat perfectly still and tried to relax, but felt his gaze return to her as they rode along. To her dismay, the desire that she thought she'd sated in the lavatory on the plane simmered back to life. She felt foolish because she knew that Dominick was just being his teasing, flirtatious self. She kept reminding herself not to take his attention to heart, and exhaled in relief when they arrived at the Sunpiper Extreme Sports School. She put her jacket back on as they climbed from the car, glad to be back under wraps for the time being.

Violet recognized the front of the building and the lobby from the pictures on their Web site. It was basically a huge arena with climbing walls and other interactive games, detailed with lots of neon. High-energy music thumped in the background. An expansive retail store featured all kinds of gear—one reason why Sunpiper would be a good fit for Dominick's sporting goods company, because it would give him an additional sales outlet.

"So," she whispered as they walked up to the welcome counter, "what's the plan?"

"It's simple," he said. "We're going to enroll in some of the classes and find out, firsthand, what the school is like."

Violet caught his arm, her eyes wide. "We?"

Dominick smiled. "Of course, *we.*"

Alarm seized her. "B-but I can't do extreme sports. I-I'm not even an athlete. And I'm afraid of heights."

"Even better to see how they handle beginners,"

Dominick said smoothly. He angled his head. "Come on, Vee, this is the kind of research that I need to do. You don't have to have any special athletic ability to do some of these activities. Besides, it'll be fun." His eyes danced with mischief. "You do know what fun is, don't you?"

Her mind went back to Lillian's comment that Violet didn't seem to have any fun. She wavered. Dominick was paying her to help him do research— it was the purpose of their trip after all. She was the one who couldn't seem to keep her mind on the business at hand, the one who was letting her longtime crush on him distract her.

He leaned in close. "Don't worry, Vee. I won't let anything happen to you."

Between the mesmerizing tone of his voice and his persuasive blue eyes, she was a goner. "Okay," she murmured, relenting. She only hoped that he didn't have something too extreme in mind... something that might scare her to the point of arousal.

A young man wearing a red Sunpiper T-shirt and a hat with reindeer antlers walked up to the counter. "Hi, I'm Tim. Can I help you folks?"

"Yeah," Dominick said cheerfully. "My girlfriend and I are interested in signing up for a class."

Violet jerked her head around to stare at him. *Girlfriend?*

He ignored her expression and put his arm around her shoulder. "We were thinking about couples bungee jumping."

9

ADMITTEDLY, VIOLET was so distracted by the warm weight of Dominick's arm around her shoulder that she almost missed what he'd said. But when the words sank in, she froze. *Couples bungee jumping?*

Dominick increased the pressure on her shoulder, drawing her closer to him. The scent of strong soap and talc filled her lungs, while being held against him made it harder to breathe.

"Have you jumped before?" Tim at the counter asked, reaching for forms.

"I'm an experienced jumper," Dominick said. "This will be the first time for my girlfriend."

There it was again—*girlfriend.* Her brain was sending out all kinds of confusing messages to the far reaches of her body.

"How high have you jumped?" the young man asked Dominick, in the way that men posture for bragging rights.

"Bloukrans River in South Africa is my tallest, um, *legitimate* jump."

The young man's eyes lit up. "No kidding? Dude, I hear that Bloukrans is the ultimate fall."

"Yeah, it was a good time."

"Going tandem now, huh?" Tim asked, nodding to Violet.

"That's right," Dominick said, giving her shoulders another squeeze. "What are our options?"

The guy checked his watch. "We have a bus leaving in twenty-five minutes for the last jump of the day. It's a good one, from a bridge over an intercoastal waterway about thirty miles from here. Really nice views, and we use pendulum bungee technology for a smooth ride."

"Is it a water pickup or will we be pulled back up to the bridge?" Dominick asked.

Every muscle in Violet's body clenched in terror at the thought of slowly being hauled back up to the jumping-off point. Dominick must have felt her response because his hand lightly stroked her collarbone.

"It's a water pickup," Tim confirmed. "It's a sweet jump for a first-timer."

Dominick nodded. "Sounds good." He looked down at her. "Right, honey?"

She could only manage a tremulous smile.

"Great," Tim said. "I just need for you to fill out the paperwork and a form of payment." He leaned forward and looked over the counter at their feet. "It's a good idea to wear athletic shoes. If you don't have any with you, there's a decent selection in our store." He gave Violet's black suit the once-over. "And you might want to wear something more casual."

Her mouth watered to say that she'd dressed for business, thank you very much, not for being dangled upside down on a big rubber band.

"Thanks," Dominick said, then dropped his arm from her shoulder to remove his wallet and slide his credit card across the counter.

Violet missed his arm around her, but it allowed her mind to fully function again. "Excuse me. How high is this jump?" she asked.

"About two hundred feet," the guy said with a grin. "Long enough for you to enjoy the fall, but short enough to give you a nice rebound."

Violet's throat contracted. "The length of two football fields?" she asked Dominick.

"Relax, you'll love it," he assured her.

But the paperwork didn't help her to relax, especially the waiver form. *The participant is aware that bungee jumping is a calculated risk sport with inherent dangers, including serious injury or death, that no amount of care, instruction or expertise can eliminate.*

"Don't worry," Dominick whispered in her ear, "I'll check all the equipment myself."

Violet signed her name with a shaky hand, but her heart was clicking double-time. She wasn't sure what scared her the most—the thought of jumping off something that wasn't on fire, or how her body would react to the certain fear.

After the forms were filled out, Tim weighed each of them and recorded it on the paperwork, then told them where to meet the bus.

"Sorry about the whole boyfriend-girlfriend thing," Dominick said as they walked across the lobby to the entrance of the retail store. "It just seemed more believable."

"That woman at the café didn't find it so believable," she said lightly.

He frowned, then an amused expression came over his face. "Why, Vee, if I didn't know better, I'd think you were jealous."

Her face heated.

He winked. "But of course, I do know better."

His comment left her feeling out of sorts. She didn't know whether to feel flattered or offended at his inference that she didn't have the capacity to be jealous.

Bemused, she followed him into the gear store that featured more neon and more pulse-pounding music. Dominick surveyed the showroom, nodding his approval. "They could use some Burns apparel, but otherwise, not a bad selection."

They went to the shoe section and Dominick picked out styles for each of them to try. Violet felt shy—trying on shoes together seemed like such an intimate act. She had to hold herself in check. Dominick was so appealing, it would be easy for her to fall into the trap of feeling like his girlfriend.

At his urging, she also tried on cargo pants and moisture-wicking shirts for the jump and, more mysteriously, "for future activities." She stealthily snagged an athletic bra to take into the changing room with her. She handed the tags to a clerk as she decided which items fit, and by the time she emerged in her new clothes, Dominick had already paid for her items and his. He was dressed similarly in long sturdy pants and a lightweight shirt. She had comfortable clothes at home for her yoga classes, but felt out of place in these hi-tech, rugged garments. Dominick's gaze roved over her, but she couldn't tell if his smile was in appreciation or amusement.

"We'd better get going," he said.

The bus ride was nerve-wracking, if only because everyone else seemed more excited about the impending jump than she was. The only upside was that Dominick sat close and kept reassuring her that everything was going to be okay. Her heartbeat raced and her breathing felt compromised. By the time they unloaded on the bridge where the bungee operation was set up, she could hardly move. Just being on the narrow bridge and feeling the openness around her was enough to make her light-headed.

"Everyone has the jitters the first time," Dominick

said, sliding his arm around her waist to propel her forward. "It's okay to be afraid."

"You're not," she murmured.

"I always get a case of the nerves before a jump. Without fear, you wouldn't get an adrenaline rush, and that's the fun of it."

She was starting to think that her idea of fun did not mesh with the rest of the world's. In the letter she'd written in college, she had craved excitement, but maybe this was going overboard. She pressed a hand to her heated face. She was feeling…edgy… tense…stimulated.

"What do you think of the class so far?" she asked Dominick, trying to steer the conversation back to business long enough to take her mind off of what she was about to do.

"So far, so good," he said. "But I want to see what kind of instructions are given by the jump master here at the bridge."

They gathered in a group while the jump master, a woman named Natalie, welcomed them and asked if anyone in the class was a first-timer. Violet gingerly raised her hand.

"Very good. Are you jumping solo?" the woman asked.

"Tandem," Dominick spoke up.

"Any other tandem jumpers?"

There were two other couples jumping tandem, and

Natalie decided they would all go last. Violet watched while the woman explained about the ankle harnesses and how the equipment was attached to the bridge.

"Don't look down," she warned with a laugh. "Look straight ahead when you approach the edge, then the group and I will count you down to jump." She stepped up on a crate to demonstrate. "Then lean forward, and jump out and away from the bridge. Those of you going solo, put your arms out like a bird." She jumped off the crate, exaggerating good form. When she landed, she straightened and grinned. "And those of you going tandem, hold on to each for dear life."

Violet's stomach churned as the other two couples twined hands, kissed and generally made eyes at each other. Suddenly she felt Dominick's hand clasp hers. When she looked up, he winked as if to say, "just for appearances."

"Don't worry," Natalie continued. "You're not going to hit the water and you're not going to bounce back up and hit the bridge. Just scream your head off and have fun. When you stop bouncing, you'll be close enough to the water that our ground crew will move an air mattress underneath you and I'll lower you onto it from up here. Any questions?"

After a couple of questions about freestyling from some of the more experienced jumpers, everyone started lining up. When a breeze blew across the bridge, Violet swayed, and Dominick caught her arm.

"Just hang on to me," he said.

She did, grabbing a fistful of his shirt to steady herself. But as each jumper was fastened into the ankle harnesses and sent off the edge by a boisterous group countdown, her anxiety ratcheted higher. Many people in the group peered over the railing to watch the jumpers, but she couldn't bring herself to get that close. Fear wallowed in her stomach…and desire hummed in her sex. She flicked out her tongue to whisk away the perspiration beaded on the rim of her lip.

Finally when it was down to the three couples going tandem, Dominick moved her closer to the platform.

"I don't think I can do this," she said, shaking her head.

"Of course you can," he said in a soothing voice. "You'll be in good hands."

She closed her eyes briefly. He wasn't helping to calm her nerves.

She watched as the first couple was readied for their jump. They each had a set of harnesses fastened to their ankles, and the bungee cord itself was heavier and thicker to support their combined weight. They stood at the edge of the platform and wrapped their arms around each other. When the couple was ready, the jump master counted them down and they sprang off together with a triumphant whoop.

Violet's stomach flipped—both at the thought that their turn was coming and at the realization of how close to Dominick she was going to be. Moisture pooled at the juncture of her thighs and her limbs felt weak.

Within a few minutes, the empty cord was hauled up and attached to the next couple. They kissed passionately as Natalie counted them down, then they pushed off together and disappeared over the edge.

"We're up," Dominick said, urging her forward to step onto the platform. Violet's breasts and sex felt heavy and tingly. She shook her head and turned to face him. "I don't think I can do it."

"Yes, you can," he said with a little smile. He clasped her upper arms. "I told you I won't let anything happen to you. Don't you trust me?"

Violet bit her lip and nodded. She just didn't trust herself.

"Then let's do this," he said, walking onto the platform and pulling her along by her hand. "Don't look down, concentrate on breathing."

The sense of having nothing around her triggered a falling sensation. Gripped with terror, she had to fight the impulse to fall to her knees and crawl back to the bus. Dominick must have sensed how close she was to mutiny because he held her gaze locked with his until the empty cord was hauled back up.

"Relax," he said, rubbing her arms. "You're with me now."

If only, she thought fleetingly.

"Ready?" Natalie asked.

"Hang on," Dominick said to Violet, then he knelt to inspect the mechanism that fastened the cord to the bridge. Seemingly satisfied, he stood. "We're ready."

Natalie smiled. "Hold up your pants legs, please."

They obliged and the woman crouched to fasten the harnesses around each of their ankles. When she'd finished, Dominick double-checked the bindings himself. The breeze picked up, whistling through Violet's ears. She clutched at his shoulders, now in a full panic, and the reassuring squeeze he gave her behind only made things worse. Her thighs were wet from the sensual lubrication her body was producing in response to the fear coursing through her veins. When Dominick wrapped his arms around her and pulled her body snug against his, she sucked in a sharp breath at the way their bodies fit together, soft into hard.

"Put your arms around me," he ordered.

She did, encountering lots of scary, firm muscle.

"Tighter," he urged. "Like you mean it."

She swallowed hard and tightened her grip. Her head came to just under his chin. She could feel his heart beating beneath her cheek, calm and steady. She sank into him, drawing on his physical strength.

"Okay, folks," Natalie said. "This is as easy as falling in love."

Violet closed her eyes at the irony of the comment.

The notion that Dominick Burns could ever fall in love with her would be laughable—if she could pull enough air into her lungs to actually laugh.

"On one," Natalie shouted. "Three!"

"Oh, God, oh, God, oh, God," Violet cried, clinging to him like a vise.

"Two!"

"Some people do this naked," he murmured into her ear.

His comment shocked her just enough to distract her for a split second.

"One—jump!"

Violet felt Dominick's muscles bunch. She wished she could say she tried to help him propel them off the platform, but frankly, she just buried her head in his chest and fell after him. There was a heart-stopping few seconds of weightlessness, then gravity took hold and they plummeted like stones.

They were going to die. As the wind rushed by them, her life flashed before her eyes—the things that she hadn't gotten to do… *There lies Violet Summerlin, she had a well-spent youth.*

Dominick shouted with pleasure. "Woo-hoo! Vee, lift your head! This is great!"

But her neck was too weak and her lungs seemed to be collapsing. Finally when all the air had been squeezed out, she opened her mouth and dragged in a breath, enough to fuel a blood-curdling scream that reverberated in her ears. His laughter blended with her shrieks. At long last, they seemed to be slowing, and Violet opened her eyes to see blotches of colors racing by. Completely disoriented, she gulped to regulate her breathing.

"Open your eyes, Vee! This is fun!"

She tried to lift her head, but centrifugal force and fear held her against his chest. They came almost to a complete stop, then she felt a tug on her ankles, and they were bouncing back up again. She dug her fingers into his back and hung onto him as if her life depended on it. Her sex throbbed as the sensation of free-falling zeroed in on her engorged erogenous zones. The rebound was short, and then they were falling again, much more slowly. Finally they settled into a light bounce, swinging back and forth, hanging upside down. She opened her eyes and slowly things came into focus, her breathing echoing in her ears.

"You did it," Dominick said, laughter in his voice.

She lifted her head. "I did it."

He lowered his mouth to hers for a quick, celebratory kiss that ended before she could register it. She blinked, her jaw loose with surprise. It was a spontaneous act, she reasoned. It wasn't supposed to mean anything.

But little did he know that she had been dreaming of that kiss for almost a year, since she'd first met him. And right now it was like breathing fresh air as the fire smoldered in her body. Even as they stopped swinging and were lowered slowly onto a large air mattress, her vital signs were on the rise. When they untangled their bodies and were disengaged from the bungee cord, her heart was still racing almost as fast as when they first jumped off the platform. During the ride back to the Sunpiper Extreme Sports School parking lot, she smiled at Dominick and told him she was fine, but she couldn't seem to calm the storm raging inside her. The memory of having her body pressed up against his, the adrenaline flowing through her, the fleeting kiss…

She was, she conceded on the ride back to the hotel, ready to blow.

"You were a trooper," Dominick said enthusiastically as they climbed higher in the glass elevator. "Are you sure you're okay?"

Violet was bracing herself against the handrails in the elevator, facing toward the doors. Her breathing was ragged and her legs felt shaky. But she couldn't look at him, afraid that her unchecked desire for him showed all over her freckled face. "I'm fine," she murmured. "Just…tired."

When the elevator doors opened, she hurried off and down the hall to their room. She had the key out and the door to the suite open before he could catch up with her. The spacious room was now bathed in low light because the setting sun had moved out of the easterly view.

"Hey, hey, where's the fire?" Dominick asked, catching her arm before she could escape to her room.

Violet looked up at him and swallowed a groan. The man was simply too sexy for words. And this kind of proximity made her think about dangerous things.

"Thank you for being such a good sport," Dominick said. "Taking the class helped me to see the inner workings of the school." He reached for her hand and twined her fingers. "And it wouldn't have been nearly as fun without you, Vee."

Her heart tripped faster and she tried to pull her hand from his, but he held her fast.

"Vee…"

When she turned back, he lowered his mouth to hers. But this time, it wasn't celebratory and it wasn't quick. His lips were warm and wet and hungry, unleashing the raging desire she'd so carefully kept at bay. Violet opened her mouth to him, and felt herself being pulled over the edge.

She'd already survived one free fall. This one might be a lot more dangerous, but promised to be a lot more fun.

_10_

VIOLET SANK INTO Dominick as the kiss became more frenzied. All the tension, exhilaration and fear of the last few hours collided with her fantasies of Dominick over the past year to fuel her mouth and her hands. She moaned and slipped her fingers under his T-shirt to knead the thick muscles along his spine. He pulled away long enough to lift his shirt over his head, then tug at the hem of hers. Without hesitation, she raised her arms and allowed him to remove her shirt. The chill from the air-conditioning raised goose bumps on her arms, sending a shiver across her shoulders.

He lowered his mouth to her neck, then to her collarbone while massaging little circles into her lower back.

Violet couldn't believe this was happening, but didn't want to stop to question the sensual assault on her body. When he unhooked the athletic bra that restrained her breasts, she sighed in relief at having them unbound. They were heavy with need, the tips hardened to dark pink points. He pushed his hands into her hair, freeing her ponytail and sending her unruly hair falling around her shoulders. A bout of shyness struck her when he held her at arm's length— she was so pale she fairly glowed in the dark. But the look in his hooded eyes was gratifying.

"Vee," he said, his voice full of wonder. "You're beautiful. Let me see the rest of you."

She removed her tennis shoes, then stood and held his gaze while she slowly unfastened the cargo pants, then stripped out of them along with her panties. When his eyes swept over her from head to toe in silence, she was afraid she'd done something wrong…or moved too fast…or wasn't his type. But then he groaned and pulled her close, running his hands down her back and over her hips.

Through his pants, the hard ridge of his erection pressed against her stomach. Impatient to have him naked, she tugged at his waistband. He kicked off his shoes, then unbuttoned his pants and pushed them down. When his erection sprang free, thick and hard, she was struck with the realization that it was really going to happen—she was going to have sex with Dominick. All the times she'd fantasized about being with him, she'd never dreamed it might actually happen. Feeling his warm, naked flesh under her fingers was surreal…more amazing than anything she'd ever concocted in her head.

He stopped long enough to retrieve a condom

from his wallet before stepping out of his pants. Then he picked her up, lifting her onto the kitchen bar at her back and kissed her wildly, slanting his mouth over hers and stabbing his tongue inside.

He broke away only to dip his head and draw a pert nipple into his mouth, massaging her breast. Violet moaned and leaned her head back, arching into him. The pleasure was almost unbearable... being kissed like this, and knowing it was Dominick. He gave the other breast equal, exquisite treatment. She drove her hands into his hair, urging him on. He suckled her until she cried out with pleasure. She could feel her own wetness, smell her own musky scent—her body was calling out to his.

He pulled back and tore open the condom package, then rolled the condom on. Violet scooted to the edge of the counter and looped her arms around his neck. He kissed her hard and braced his hands on her waist. When he pushed the head of his cock inside her, she sucked in a sharp breath. She could tell from his disjointed breathing that he was restraining himself. Inch by inch he filled her until he was fully sheathed.

"Ahh...you're so wet," he rasped, then found a long, slow rhythm, moving in and out of her with powerful, deep strokes. Violet had never felt a sensation so intense....

...until he used his thumb to strum the core of her

desire. The concentrated pleasure began coaxing the orgasm she'd nursed all afternoon to the surface, and loosened her tongue. She sighed into Dominick's neck and murmured naughty, sexy things about how good he felt filling her up, and how he was going to make her come if he kept it up. The words came unbidden and shocked her, giving her a glimpse of another Violet, a sexually confident version of herself that no man had ever been able to draw to the surface.

Dominick groaned and worked her clit, urging her on. The warm vibration deep inside of her swirled tighter and tighter. She wrapped her legs around his waist and squeezed as his ministrations took her over the edge in a cascade of fireworks. The climax was so forceful, she called out his name as her body quaked with spasms. "Dominick…oh, yes…Dominick…Dominick."

From his ragged breathing, she knew that he, too, was close to orgasm. He cupped her hips, driving in and out of her, then tensed and came in a long, guttural release. "Vee…Vee…ahh." His body shuddered over and over until finally he stilled inside her.

Holding his head against her breasts, Violet felt utterly sated as her breathing returned to normal. But deep inside, some small part of her knew that this was just a one-time thing. Dominick had lots of women, all of them more exciting than her. And since she'd had a crush on him for so long, having sex again probably wasn't a sound idea. The last thing she wanted to do was fall in love with Dominick Burns and get her heart broken for Christmas.

A noise intruded into the silence. The sound of scratching and whining came from her bedroom door. Winslow had probably heard them and was no doubt bored. Violet prodded Dominick with her finger.

"Hmm?" he asked, raising his head.

"I think Winslow needs me."

He made an irritated noise and pulled away from her. "Okay. But we need to talk about this."

"Nothing to talk about," she said, effecting a breezy tone. She slid down from the counter and began gathering her clothes. She had to put some space between them, to be alone to absorb the enormity of what had just happened—namely, sex more earth-shattering than even Dr. Alexander had made seem possible in her lectures.

Violet's legs were unstable, but she forced herself to straighten and look at him. "Thank you—it was very nice. But I hope it doesn't change our working relationship."

DOMINICK BLINKED. He prided himself on pleasing his lovers, but he'd never been *thanked*. And Violet's prim delivery erased any smugness he might've otherwise felt.

It was very nice—what the hell did *that* mean? He

wasn't in the habit of keeping score, but he could say, without reservation, that making it with Violet ranked at the top of *his* sexual experiences.

Maybe things had unfolded more quickly than he'd intended, but that was only because he'd thought he was going to die if he didn't bury himself inside her. He'd been planning to take his time on the second go-around. His cock was already hard for her again. How could it not be with her standing there nude like some kind of goddess, with her red-gold hair spilling over her shoulders? The woman's amazing breasts alone were enough to keep him entertained for months.

He shook his head, confounded at her reaction. "Uh, no, this won't affect our working relationship."

"Good," she said.

He scrambled for something to put them back on neutral ground. "Let's get cleaned up and go out for dinner."

"I don't think so." Violet pulled on her clothes, putting that mind-blowing body back under wraps. "I have some phone calls to return and I'm really tired. I think I'll just get room service and maybe take Winslow for a walk." She looked up at him. "What's on the agenda for tomorrow?"

His mind swirled in surprise, and he gave a little laugh at the fact that they were talking about business while he was standing there stark naked. Apparently, she was underwhelmed. "I guess we should meet for breakfast at the café, and make plans for the day then."

"What time?"

He held up his hands, at a loss. "How about nine?"

"Okay." She gathered up her incredible hair and captured it into its perennial ponytail with the rubber band he'd removed. Then she gave him a perfectly cheerful smile. "Have a good evening."

He half expected her to add "Mr. Burns," but she didn't. Instead, she turned and disappeared into her room. From the noises coming from the other side of the door, that ridiculous excuse for a dog was pretty damn happy to see her.

Dominick bit back a curse and picked up his clothes as he made his way back to his own room with its big, lonely bed. He showered slowly, his mind reeling over what they'd just done. His body was still burning for Violet. He wanted to explore every creamy inch of her, wanted to taste her abundance of musky nectar that had made sliding into her body such exquisite torture. And who could've guessed that the sweet girl who wanted world peace for Christmas could talk like a courtesan in the throes of passion? It was as if she'd become a different woman in his arms. When he started to get another hard-on, he turned the water to cold and stood under it, feeling like a schoolboy.

His bad mood persisted as he dressed for dinner.

As he unpacked his suitcase, he came across the letter that Violet had written. He unfolded the pink pages and reread the words, feeling contrite when he got to the part about the guys being done before she could get her shirt off. What Violet probably didn't realize was that the young men were so hot for her smoking body, they couldn't hold back.

Dominick frowned—like him.

Feeling decidedly crabby, he stashed the letter and left the room, casting a longing glance at Violet's closed bedroom door on his way out. He found a lively place on the beach to eat that was crammed full of tanned, gorgeous, half-naked women dancing and laughing, drinking and flirting. Many of them came up to him at the bar and ground their bodies against his, letting other men lick salt off their cleavage while doing tequila shots.

These women, he thought crossly, knew how to have fun.

So why did his mind keep creeping back to the pale, freckled woman who lived in turtlenecks and preferred a quiet night alone to a night out with him?

Dominick downed the rest of his vodka tonic and signaled the bartender for another. As his ire rose, so did his lust for Violet. It was maddening to think that she'd been right under his nose for a year, smoldering...

He pursed his mouth. So sex on a counter in a hotel room after bungee jumping off a bridge wasn't enough to satisfy the little minx who fantasized about exciting sex?

There was only one solution, he thought as he picked up his refilled glass and drank deeply.

Tomorrow, he'd simply have to up his game.

11

Three days until Christmas

VIOLET WAS A nervous wreck as she made her way to the beachside café where she and Dominick had agreed to meet for breakfast. She'd barely slept last night, replaying every erotic detail in her head until the scene was burned into her memory. She'd heard him return around two in the morning and, judging from the amount of noise he'd made getting to his bedroom, he'd been lit up like a Christmas tree. Since he'd still been sporting a hard-on when she'd last seen him, she assumed he'd gone out to find someone with whom to party and to…wrap up the evening. Apparently she hadn't been woman enough to satisfy him completely.

His bedroom door had been closed when she'd left early this morning to take a walk on the beach, was still closed when she returned, and was still closed when she'd left again. She and Winslow had taken the long way around to the café specifically so that she wouldn't run into Dominick before she was ready to face him.

Between suppressing yawns, she rehearsed a casual smile for the moment she saw him. She couldn't let him know how much last night had meant to her. He would think she was beyond pitiful.

Winslow trotted next to her enthusiastically, having spent a restful night curled up to her in bed. The little dog snored like a Saint Bernard, but she couldn't blame her sleeplessness on him entirely. She'd been wide awake, wallowing in self-recrimination. Over the past year, Dominick had evolved into her best customer. And despite what he'd said about sex not changing their working relationship, she didn't see how it couldn't. Once you'd seen a person naked, things changed. Yet she was nothing if not practical. At this point, all she could do to mitigate the situation was to employ damage control and get back to business.

She was wearing another black pantsuit and her loafers, but in deference to the heat, had donned one of Lillian's sleeveless colorful blouses. As she approached the café, she spotted Dominick sitting at the table where they'd had lunch yesterday. He was dressed in cargo shorts and a T-shirt that hugged his broad shoulders. He wore sunglasses and was slumped in the chair, massaging his temples. Her body reacted predictably, shamelessly loosening and expanding.

She slowed, her chest prickling with anxiety. But Winslow saw him and pulled against his leash, barking furiously.

Dominick looked up and frowned—but at her or the dog, she couldn't tell. When she walked up, he took off his glasses and rubbed his eyes with thumb and forefinger. "Good morning, Vee."

"Good morning," she said, giving him her practiced smile.

He nodded to Winslow and winced with every bark. "Does he have to be so loud?"

She looped the leash around the leg of her chair, then crouched to quiet the little dog. "He's just happy to see you," she said lightly.

"So that's his friendly growl?" Dominick asked dryly, setting aside his sunglasses.

It was impossible to look at him and not be reminded of where his lips and hands had touched her last night. Her nipples hardened in vivid recollection. "Did you have a nice dinner?"

The waitress appeared before he could respond. Violet ordered yogurt and orange juice. Dominick ordered a packet of powdered aspirin and a bottle of Gatorade. When the woman left, he leaned back in his chair and gave a rueful laugh. "I don't remember the food, but I definitely drank too much. I'm sorry if I woke you when I came in."

"You didn't," she lied.

"So you got some rest?"

"Yes." She hoped he didn't notice the dark circles under her eyes that powder couldn't quite conceal.

"So, how do you feel the morning after?"

She jerked her head up.

A mischievous smile lifted his mouth. "After the bungee jump, I mean."

"Oh. A little sore," she confessed. Although the slight aches in her hip and thigh muscles were probably attributable to their carnal exercises.

"Ready for some more?"

Violet swallowed hard. "More what?"

"Classes at Sunpiper. I thought we'd try something else today…if you're up to it."

"Um…sure," she said, remembering her vow to get back to business. It was the reason Dominick had brought her, after all. "As long as it's not anything too…extreme."

"Something tells me you have a pretty high threshold for excitement," he said.

Perplexed by his comment, she tingled under his gaze.

The waitress brought their order, and Dominick held up the packet of aspirin. "I need a couple of hours to feel human again before we get our adrenaline going."

"That's fine," Violet said, eager to postpone the

outing for as long as possible. "I spotted a row of boutiques nearby. I'll take care of finishing the shopping on your list before we leave and send the gifts to my office."

"I'll go with you," he said. "Maybe I'll pick up on some of your shopping tips and be able to do my own from now on."

Violet nodded and stirred her yogurt. So he was already planning to curtail the services he purchased from her. A taut silence stretched between them until it vibrated, reminding her of the tension leading up to an orgasm. They shifted in their chairs, moved their feet. She took small bites and cast about for a neutral topic.

"The weather is nice," they said in unison.

She smiled and he grinned back, easing the awkwardness. "But it's hard to get into the Christmas spirit when it's so warm and sunny," Violet added.

"I think that's why I like it down here," he said. "I can forget about the holiday."

Violet blinked. "You don't like Christmas?"

He shrugged. "I don't have anything against Christmas. It's great for kids. I just don't understand the fuss that adults make over it."

Violet looked back to her yogurt, suddenly homesick.

"Did I say something wrong?"

"No," she said with a quick smile. "When I was a

girl, I always dreamed of having one of those magical Christmases with my parents, with a big tree and snow and Christmas carols."

"Your parents weren't around for Christmas?"

She shook her head.

His forehead creased in thought. "Was this year supposed to be your magical Christmas?"

She fidgeted in her chair. "I've outgrown all that silliness." It was time to let go of the fantasy she'd concocted in her head. It was never going to happen.

"When I was growing up, my mother made a big deal out of decorating the tree and making cookies and wrapping gifts." His eyes grew warm. "I guess that's why I usually find something to do over the holidays. Without family, it just isn't the same."

His words tugged on her heart. "Do you mind if I ask what happened to your folks?"

"Cancer took my mom. And my dad died of a heart attack less than a year later." Dominick's smile was sad. "I always figured he died of a broken heart."

"Sounds like my grandparents," she murmured. "I'm so sorry."

"Me, too," he said, then averted his gaze and polished off his Gatorade, as if eager to change the subject and get going.

Violet finished eating quickly, watching Dominick from under her lashes. It was understandable why he didn't enjoy Christmas, but profoundly sad.

Yet it explained why he was willing to pay someone else to do his gift-buying, and why he wasn't returning to Atlanta until the day after Christmas. It also made her wonder if, despite his constant female entourage, Dominick was lonely.

But she discarded that idea as she swallowed the last of her juice. Dominick was sitting there with her, but his mind was elsewhere. He drummed idly on the table and glanced around, already bored being in one place…bored with her. The man's personality and energy level were simply too big to be limited to one city, to one business, to one woman. A man like Dominick didn't get lonely.

Violet quashed a pang of disappointment, chastising herself for entertaining, even for a second, the idea that she and Dominick could be anything but…this.

"Ready?" he asked, obviously anxious to get started. He tossed cash on the table to cover their meal.

She nodded and unhooked Winslow's leash, pulling it short enough to keep the dog close to her feet as they walked toward the street where she'd found the boutiques. Dominick didn't seem to be in the mood this morning to be bitten.

DOMINICK THOUGHT that walking next to Violet would be easier than sitting across from her—he still couldn't touch her, but at least he could be closer to her. Except that anytime he got too close, that damned dog growled at him. So, from more than arm's-length distance, Dominick tried to forget how much his head pounded and focused on drinking in the sight of Violet as she moved.

She walked with an economy of motion, taking up no more space than absolutely necessary, keeping her elbows in, her stride controlled. Yet there was no shyness in her posture—her head was up and her shoulders were back, providing a nice framework for the magnificent breasts he knew were in hiding beneath that black suit jacket. Remembering the hardened tips in his mouth, his cock began to swell.

"This looks promising," Violet said, stopping on the sidewalk.

Dominick eyed the store dubiously. The windows were chock full of glass knickknacks and decorative bric-a-brac. "Is this the kind of place I'd have to visit if I did my own shopping?"

"As long as your gift list is ninety percent female," she said pointedly.

"Touché," he said with a grin. "Okay, show me how it's done."

She opened the door and asked the clerk if she could bring Winslow inside. The young woman smiled and nodded yes. Once they were in the shop, Violet looped the leash around her wrist, then pulled out her PDA and punched in few commands.

Dominick looked over her shoulder. "What are you doing?"

"You have four people left to buy for—Heather, Mia, Sandy and Bethany. I'm double-checking your cumulative gift list."

His eyebrows went up. "You keep track of what I've given to each person this year?"

She nodded. "That way I don't inadvertently send a duplicate." When the list came up, she read from it. "Your gifts for Heather to-date have been chocolates for Valentine's Day and an iPod in April."

Dominick felt sheepish. "She's…young." A cheerleader at Georgia State, in fact. The woman could do a Chinese split, but she didn't stir him like Violet did.

"Do you have something specific in mind?" she asked, breaking into his musing.

"No. What would you suggest?" He hadn't seen Heather in months. This was more of a parting gift than anything else.

"The key to gift-giving is simply to think of something that the person would like, but would never buy for himself or herself. How about a purse compact?" She picked up a lovely sterling compact studded with crystals.

He frowned. "What exactly is a compact?"

She smiled and opened it. "It's a mirror."

"Perfect," he said, relieved. This wasn't so hard.

She set the item on the counter, then leaned over to peer at a round-faced fabric doll in a faded box. "How much is this doll?" she asked the clerk.

The woman shook her head. "Sorry. It belongs to the owner and isn't for sale."

Violet made a rueful noise.

"What is it?" Dominick asked.

"It's a vintage Little People doll," Violet said. "A man in Georgia created them—they were the precursor to the Cabbage Patch Kids dolls before they were mass produced." She smiled. "When I was seven, they were all the rage."

"Did you have one?" he asked.

She gave a little laugh. "Oh, no. My grandparents couldn't afford one. But they did take me to north Georgia to the clinic."

"Clinic?"

"Where the dolls were born and taken care of before they were adopted out," she explained with a smile.

He shook his head. "Boys' toys are so much simpler. When I was seven, all I wanted was a skateboard."

Violet nodded her agreement, then turned her attention back to her PDA. "Next on the list is Mia. You sent her chocolates for Valentine's Day and flowers in July."

He looked around the sparkly, crowded shop and lifted his hands. "I'm at a loss."

"What's she like?" Violet asked.

"Um…" Dominick frowned, unable at the moment

to even conjure up a mental image of the woman. She was in pharmaceutical sales…maybe. Then he snapped his fingers. "She always smells good." Not as good as Violet, though, who smelled like—he leaned closer to her ponytail—gingerbread cookies.

The dog barked loudly and Dominick's head snapped back.

Oblivious, Violet reprimanded the dog, who whimpered and moved closer to her, watching Dominick with his dark little eyes.

She swung her aqua-colored gaze to Dominick. "How about a perfume decanter?"

"Which is…?"

She picked up a small pink glass bottle with a stopper. "To hold her favorite perfume."

"Perfect," he agreed. Another parting gift. Now that he thought about it, most of his year-end gifts were symbolic, wiping the relationship slate clean.

Violet set aside the perfume bottle, then consulted the list. "You gave Sandy chocolates for Valentine's Day, flowers in May and season tickets to the symphony in October."

"She's my housekeeper," he explained. "I've known her since I was a kid. Great lady."

Violet's expression softened. "That's nice. Do you have any idea of what you'd like to give her?"

"Something indulgent," he said. "The woman spends way too much time trying to take care of me."

Violet walked over to a rack of garments hanging against a wall. "How about a cashmere bathrobe? I can't think of anything more indulgent."

Dominick touched the ultrasoft pale gray fabric, noticing the elegance of Violet's hands. Her fingers were long, her nails bare and neat. She wore a ring on her right hand that looked antique—he'd bet it had belonged to her grandmother.

"The robe is perfect," he agreed, thinking that Sandy would be at a loss for words over the extravagance. Appreciation welled in his chest. "Thank you, Vee. It means a lot to me to be able to give Sandy something special."

She smiled, removing the robe from the hanger. "That's what you pay me for."

He followed her to the counter to purchase the items, disturbed by Violet's reminder that she worked for him. When they left the store with the gifts, he caught her arm. "Vee…last night in the hotel room, you didn't feel pressured to…" He cleared his throat, feeling like an idiot.

"No," she said quickly, her cheeks turning bright pink. "I wanted it to happen, Dominick."

"Good," he said, feeling relieved…and awkward. This woman was probably the most shy, inexperienced woman he'd ever slept with, yet she made *him* feel inept.

She gestured to a jewelry shop two doors down.

"Jewelry for Bethany, right? We can knock out the last gift."

He paused, suddenly uncomfortable with the thought of picking out jewelry for another woman with Violet in tow. "Maybe I should take care of this one myself."

She raised her eyebrows. "Oh. Okay. Why don't I take Winslow for a little walk up the street? Take your time."

Dominick watched her walk away and frowned. He'd rather go with her. But instead, he pushed open the door of the jewelry store. At the sight of case after case of engagement rings, though, he nearly had a panic attack. He quickly moved to the more innocuous cases of earrings, then scratched his head. Were Bethany's ears pierced? He hadn't spent a lot of time looking at the woman's lobes. Maybe he'd be better off buying a bracelet as a breakup gift. But even a bracelet seemed a little...intimate. Then he caught sight of the watch case and brightened. A watch was jewelry, but not.

Perfect.

He selected a feminine but plain style and paid for it, eager to get back to Violet. Then a thought popped into his head—should he buy a Christmas gift for Vee?

He stopped near the door and peered into a case that happened to contain rings. A delicate gold filigree band caught his eye—it would suit Vee's elegant hand.

"Would you like to see a ring, sir?" the clerk asked.

Dominick looked up at the man's knowing smile and straightened. "Uh, no, thanks." Then he bolted for the door, pulling his hand down his face when he reached the sidewalk. What was he thinking? Even without a diamond, women attached meaning to rings. And a ring would be wildly inappropriate for what he and Vee had.

He squinted. Which was…what? The sex had certainly blurred the lines—at least for him.

Dominick turned and caught sight of Violet a few yards away, crouched down, face-to-face with the ugly little dog, roughing up its fur and talking to it as if it were a child. Her devotion to a client's dog was admirable—and indicative of the way she lived her life, he realized. She was guileless and didn't have an angle. It was…refreshing.

She looked up and waved, then walked toward him, coaxing the dog along. "All done?" she asked.

He nodded as an alien feeling zigzagged through his chest—probably just indigestion. "Uh, yeah."

"Great. There's an overnight service center at the hotel. When we get back, I'll send everything to Lillian and she'll make sure the gifts are wrapped and delivered before Christmas Eve."

"Sounds good," he said, still shaken by this rampant…*affection* that he seemed to be developing for Violet. "Do you have your Christmas shopping done?"

She nodded and dropped her gaze, suddenly fascinated by the handle of the leash she held. "I gave my parents their gifts before I left." Then she looked up. "Ready to go?"

"Yeah, sure."

They walked back to the hotel in relative silence, except for the occasional growl from the Pekingese when Dominick strayed too close to Violet.

"I'm going to leave him at the doggie spa this afternoon," she said, brushing at the orange hair on her black pants. "He needs to be groomed."

"He needs an attitude adjustment," Dominick said wryly.

Violet laughed. "I'll have to let them know when I'll be picking him up. How long will we be gone today, doing…research?"

Dominick hesitated. He was having second thoughts about his plan to seduce her again by way of adrenaline rush. He didn't have anything to offer Violet in terms of a commitment, and despite the fantasies she'd written down, she was the kind of woman who needed—who deserved—something more than just a few nights of illicit sex. She belonged back home with her parents, celebrating that magical Christmas that she'd always dreamed of.

But when she lifted her heavy-lidded gaze to his, her tongue flicked out to moisten her parted pink lips, and her face was flushed from more than the Florida heat.

She wanted this, too, he realized as lust arrowed straight to his groin.

"As long as it takes," he answered, half to himself.

12

TANDEM PARAGLIDING, Violet learned, consisted of two people strapped into individual sling harnesses, which allowed them to sit—one in front of the other—and use a wide, narrow parachute-like "wing" to capture and ride the wind.

"I've stayed in the air for two hours lots of times," Dominick assured her as he strapped her into the harness, "but this time we'll only be up for less than an hour. It's safe and it's fun. Paragliding is as close to being a bird as a human can get."

But even following an afternoon of prep and training from Sunpiper instructors that Dominick seemed impressed with, she was trembling with fear. "I've actually never wanted to be a bird."

His laugh rumbled out, then he winked. "Once we get airborne, if you don't like it, we'll come back down, okay?"

Violet wet her lips. "Okay."

They stood on a grassy incline north of Miami amongst other students who'd taken the class. The sun was high in a sky of thin clouds and the temperature hovered in the nineties. Dominick was a certified paragliding pilot, so he was allowed to take her up using the school's equipment. Other students were either going on short solo flights or going up with qualified instructors.

A bead of sweat trickled down her neck, and a low throb pulsed in her midsection. When Dominick crouched and pulled the straps tighter over her thighs, she suppressed a moan. He glanced up at her and she knew from his slightly hooded expression that he was remembering their private adventure last night.

"Are you okay?" he asked.

She swallowed hard and nodded.

He stood and helped her with her helmet, then adjusted the chin strap and touched his finger to her nose. "I'm not going to let anything bad happen to you, Vee. Try to enjoy it."

She managed a shaky smile. Dominick was so physically commanding, he instilled confidence. Still…it was impossible to tell her body not to react to the anxiety. Beneath the rugged clothes and sports bra, her nipples were erect, and all the nerve endings in her secret places were colluding to produce an abundance of lubrication. Maybe it was some age-old response to fear, to drive women to have sex during times of crisis in order to preserve the human race. Whatever the origin, her body seemed to be preparing itself for sensual warfare.

She knew, deep down, that if she told Dominick outright that she didn't want to go, he would call off the ride. After all, their research for the class—the instruction piece—was essentially over. The paragliding trip itself was strictly a bonus…and even though her limbs were quaking at the thought of soaring high in the sky sitting in what amounted to little more than a sturdy diaper, she was drawn to it like the moth to a dangerous flame.

Like she was drawn to Dominick.

He ran his hands over her again to check the security of the straps, leaving a fiery trail on her sensitized skin. Apparently satisfied, he smiled. "Ready?"

She nodded.

"I need a Roger on that, Vee."

"Roger," she said, lifting her chin.

He grinned, then stepped behind her to strap himself into his own harness. As the pilot, Dominick would be responsible for helping to launch them safely and to control the wing once they were airborne. He had a radio to contact a leader on the ground if necessary.

"On three, we're going to run," he said in her ear. "Right foot first. As soon as you feel your feet leave the ground, sit back into your sling. Got it?"

"Roger," she said, taking a deep breath. Her heart was pounding against her breastbone like a hammer.

"Here we go—one…two…three!"

Leading with her right foot, she lumbered forward. Behind her, Dominick was matching her stride, using Kevlar cables to coax the wing off the ground and into the air. After a half-dozen steps, her feet met nothingness. Following a few seconds of abject terror, she remembered to shift her rear back into the sling. They lurched forward and her stomach pitched as the ground disappeared in front of her. And then a sensation much like riding a chairlift took hold. They were pulled higher and higher by the orange-colored wing now fully expanded above them. She felt the ascending tug on her shoulders from the harness, but her legs swung freely from the knee down.

"How're you doing up there?" Dominick called.

Violet hadn't realized she was holding her breath. She expelled a long breath through her mouth, like a Lamaze exercise, keeping her head up as the wind whooshed by her. Cold panic tickled the back of her neck.

"Talk to me, Vee."

"I'm…okay," she managed to say without moving her head.

"Just keep breathing and relax," he said. "I'm right here."

His knees nudged her behind, then clasped hold until she was cradled between his thighs.

"I got you," he said near her ear. "Just sit back and enjoy the ride."

Adrenaline flooded her chest and arms, rendering her light-headed. And having Dominick's warm body at her back only magnified the sensation of floating in a vat of liquid. She blinked several times to focus, and slowly, centimeter by centimeter, shifted her head to take in the vista before them.

It took her breath away. The horizon stretched in front of them, meeting water at several points. Below them were the tops of palm trees, sandy fields and marshland. They continued to rise, riding through the white vapor of clouds, until the ground below them lost detail and arranged itself into a grid. Dominick would be looking for thermal currents, she remembered from the training—columns of warmer and lighter air that rose naturally, to elevate them higher with less effort. Time seemed to be suspended as they floated along. Everything below them was miniature and rendered somehow less important. She felt omnipotent, watching tiny vehicles and figures moving around.

"Look to your left," he said in her ear.

When she did, she gasped. A seagull flew next to them, its dark wings moving in slow motion. Birds, too, were looking for currents to ride, she realized in awe. The white-breasted gull was their companion for several long minutes, then it suddenly dove and spiraled out of sight.

Violet let the wonder of their experience fill up her lungs. The air was cooler at this height and it was unbelievably quiet, with only the *slap, slap* of the wing above, and the swish of Dominick maneuvering the guide wires. Violet could hear her own heartbeat, her blood rushing in her ears.

"What do you think, Vee?" Dominick asked.

She closed her eyes against the rough timbre of his voice that set off new waves of vibrations through her sex. She felt so raw and so aroused, she could imagine their nude bodies joined like this, her sitting in his lap, impaled on his erection. "Mmm," she murmured.

"Gets your blood flowing, doesn't it?" he said.

She nodded. Every part of her felt engorged. She wanted the ride—the sensation—to go on forever, and at the same time she wanted it to stop. The pressure building in her womb was both exhilarating and unbearable. He banked the glider, and she realized they had turned around and were going back in the direction they'd come.

"Ready to take it up a notch?" he asked.

Violet tensed. "What do you mean?" she said over her shoulder.

"It's called a wing-over. We shift our weight from side to side and eventually swing up level with the chute. It's a blast. Just follow my lead."

She tensed, but when he squeezed her with his knees and said, "Lean right," she did.

"Now left...now right."

With every reallocation of their weight, the paraglider swung in an ever-increasing arc until they were level and, in some cases, higher than the orange wing. It felt as if they were in an adult jumper swing, bouncing from side to side. The rush was thrilling and scary and Violet found herself squealing with every swing. Gradually, he leveled them out again. "That was fun," she said over her shoulder, laughing.

He gave her a squeeze with his knees and a different kind of thrill speared through her body. They sailed along quietly for a while and suddenly landmarks started to look familiar.

"That'll do it for today," he said, and they began to descend slowly through the haze of the clouds. They drifted down so gradually, she was surprised when they were skimming the tops of palm trees, heading for a deserted field of tall, marshy grass.

"Okay, stand upright in your leg harnesses," he said.

She shifted forward, her heart vaulting to her throat at leaving the stability of the sling. She comforted herself with the knowledge that if she plummeted at this height, she was likely not to break *every* bone in her body.

"We're landing into the wind," Dominick said, "so we should have a nice, soft set-down. Your legs are going to feel like jelly, but I need for you to hit the ground running and keep going until you feel resistance from me."

She leaned forward and spread her legs shoulder-width. When she felt the grass beneath her feet, she took off running until she felt a drag on her weight. Dominick's arms came around her and they tumbled to the ground together. She landed on top of him, breathless. He was grinning, holding her tight.

"What did you think?" he asked, his blue eyes alight.

Her body was vibrating like a piano string. "I… think it was better than the bungee jump."

"So have I converted you to extreme sports?"

She moistened her lips. "I can see the healthy benefits."

"Some people go their entire lives, Vee, and never experience the thrill of having adrenaline pump through their bodies like this."

"That's…unfortunate," she agreed.

He rolled her over until she was partially beneath him. The scent of pungent earth and the tall, parched grass tickled her nose. Above her, Dominick's eyes turned smoky, fanning the flame smoldering in her stomach. A primitive longing welled in her sex.

It was involuntary, undulating her hips into his. His eyes glazed. Even through the bulky equipment, their bodies conveyed need.

He picked up her hand, then stroked her palm with

his thumb. "What do you say we stall a little while before calling the ground crew to come and get us?"

She turned her head to see if there were any houses or cars close by, but the tall grass obscured her view. "What if someone sees us?"

"What if they do?" he murmured. "You certainly have nothing to be ashamed of."

Violet flushed. The way he looked at her was like a tripwire to the volatility that had been building in her womb all day. "Okay."

Harnesses and helmets were discarded. Dominick spread out the nylon wing for them to lie on, then undressed her, paying homage to every exposed erogenous zone with blunt-tipped, calloused fingers. He released her hair, pushing his hands into it as he kissed her hungrily. She pulled at his clothes until they were skin to skin.

It was Violet's first time being nude outdoors. The sun warmed her back and buttocks, while the wind made her aware of the wetness on her thighs. The sight of her milky complexion next to his bronze body illustrated how different they were. He looked like some kind of wild animal with his shaggy mane and jutting erection. She splayed her hands over his chest, reveling in the feel of his muscles under her fingertips. The maleness of him took her breath away, made her say things she'd never uttered before.

"I want to ride you," she said, guiding him down on

the orange nylon. He didn't resist, just pulled her down with him. His breathing was ragged, his hands hurried. He reached for the condom that had been scavenged from his clothes and sheathed his raging erection. Violet straddled him and eased her body down, impaling herself on him like she'd imagined all afternoon. The fullness of him inside her made her cry out.

He closed his hands over her breasts, pulling on her nipples until they were distended and erect. "Easy," he murmured through gritted teeth.

But she was already too far gone, having been on a slow burn all day. She put her fingers to her protruding clit and, within a few seconds, the repressed orgasm came to the surface like a reawakened volcano. Intense spasms claimed her as she rocked on his body to ride out the pleasure.

DOMINICK WAS TRYING to name the U.S. presidents in order, count backwards from one hundred by multiples of nine—anything to distract his mind and body long enough to delay the orgasm building in his balls. But when Violet began contracting around him, it was as if she were milking his essence from his body. He exploded so forcefully that he bucked beneath her, which, from the happy little cries coming from her, appeared to prolong her own climax.

When their bodies quieted, she fell forward on his chest. The curtain of her red-gold hair obscured his face, but Dominick didn't have the strength to push it aside. He simply lay there inhaling her ginger-scented curls, trying to process what had just happened. He didn't have to look at a watch to know that scarcely a minute had passed since she'd climbed on him as if he were an amusement park ride.

He hadn't gotten off that quickly since his junior year of high school.

He swallowed against a parched throat, trying to silence the alarms going off in his head. Sure, she had a body that wouldn't quit, and sure, she was sweet and smart, but it was Violet Summerlin's curiosity about "exciting" sex that fueled his passion, not the woman herself.

He hoped.

Dominick reached up to uncover his face, but his hand got sidetracked by the silkiness of her luxurious hair, and inexplicably stayed there.

13

Two days until Christmas

VIOLET STARTLED awake to the sound of a buzz saw in her room, then realized it was only Winslow lying next to her, snoring. Hazy sunlight sifted through the filmy sheers on her room window. The clock read six thirty-two. Two hours and twenty-eight minutes until she met Dominick for breakfast.

She sighed and settled back on her pillow, awash with incredulity and anxiety. The sex she'd had with Dominick yesterday in the deserted field had been the most erotic experience of her life. But afterward, she had retreated from him, had bowed out of dinner to tend to Winslow so that Dominick wouldn't suspect what was happening—that despite the self-lectures, despite knowing better and despite the fact that she was headed for guaranteed heartbreak, she was well on her way to falling hopelessly in love with him.

The fact that she'd been nursing a crush on him for so long didn't help. Add to that the man was so gorgeous her vision blurred if she looked at him for too long. But what she marveled over was how he was able to pull her from her shell to try new things, how he seemed to know every button to push. It was uncanny….

But then again, Dominick probably made every woman he was with feel that way, as if he knew exactly what turned them on. He hadn't earned his playboy reputation without good reason. His gift list alone was proof that while the lucky Bethany warranted jewelry—a beautiful watch…she'd peeked before she'd dropped the gifts in the mail to Lillian—he wasn't in danger of becoming a one-woman man anytime soon. And when he did settle down, it would probably be with a muscle-ripped female athlete who scaled the sides of mountains, not a yogaphile who was scared of heights.

A snort rent the air. Winslow jarred awake and lifted his hairy head, licking his chops as his eyes blinked sleepily.

"Good morning, handsome," she said, rubbing his ears.

He made happy rumbling noises in his throat.

She wondered what it would be like to wake up lying next to Dominick, if he snored or made noises in his sleep. Derailing that futile line of thought, she swung her legs over the edge of the bed and stood for a tall stretch. Winslow lumbered to his feet then jumped off and came over to lick her feet.

She laughed, wiggling her toes. "I'm glad some-one adores me."

He looked up at her forlornly then glanced around the room, whining.

"Do you miss your mama?" she asked with a sigh. "I wonder if mama misses you." Some pet owners underestimated how traumatic it could be for animals to have their routines interrupted. Even if Winslow wouldn't "go" for Patricia Kingsbury, he was accustomed to her voice and her scent and her company.

"Let's take a walk on the beach," Violet suggested. "It'll put us both in a better frame of mind."

She pulled on a pair of shorts, a T-shirt, and the sandals she could slip off in the sand. She swept her hair back into a ponytail, thinking about how Dominick had released it from its clasp both times they'd had sex. And why not? It helped to complete her transformation, because in his arms she felt like a different woman.

I hope you find a way out of yourself.

Violet smiled at the remembered words of the lost letter. Maybe she was starting to do just that. She just hoped she wouldn't lose her heart in the process.

The letter... Now that she was actually living the fantasies she'd written about, she wished she still had it as a keepsake. It had been, after all, the catalyst for her to accept Dominick's invitation. She checked the time. Lillian was probably already in the office unless she was running errands. Violet dialed the number and Lillian answered on the second ring.

"Summerlin at Your Service, this is Lillian."

"Lillian, hi. It's Violet."

"Good morning. How's your trip going?"

Heat suffused her chest. "It's going…well…I think. I was just checking in to see how things are going there."

"Everything's great."

Violet pursed her mouth. "No problems?"

"No problems whatsoever. How's Winslow?"

She looked down at the little dog who sat at her feet with his leash in his mouth. "He's fine. We're all…fine."

"Good," Lillian said cheerfully.

"Lillian, the letter that was…misplaced. It hasn't turned up by chance, has it?"

"No, I'm sorry, it hasn't."

She fought disappointment. "That's okay, I was just checking. Call me if you need anything."

"I will."

Violet hung up the phone, bemused by the fact that her business could be operated by someone other than…her. Maybe, when she returned to Atlanta, she could ease up on her hours after all.

Winslow whined, reminding her of her promise to take a walk. She opened her bedroom door as silently as possible to find the living room empty and the door to Dominick's bedroom closed. He'd stayed out late again, until after three in the morning according to her clock. No doubt he'd found female companionship for the evening. For all she knew, he could have a woman in his bed right now. She quashed a pang of unreasonable jealousy and led Winslow out the door into the hallway. They rode down in the freight elevator and exited the hotel toward the beach.

With a breeze coming off the water, the temperature was much cooler at this early hour, but held the promise of another scorching day. Violet filled her lungs with the salt-scented air and strode onto the beach, coaxing Winslow to walk on the unfamiliar surface. He high-stepped and whined until he realized that the sand wasn't going to hurt him, then trotted ahead on his leash to explore.

Colorful rentable resort chairs and umbrellas were already being lined up and wiped off in anticipation of a busy beach crowd. It was surprising to her how many people traveled over the holidays, spent Christmas away from their home. Although she supposed everyone had their reasons.

Like her…and Dominick.

She slipped off her sandals and carried them, enjoying the feel of the sugary sand squishing between her bare toes. She moved closer to the water's edge, laughing at Winslow's alternating curiosity and terror of the waves and foam rolling in from the sea. She strolled along, dodging beachcombers, clumps of blue-green seaweed and the occasional remains of a beached jellyfish. In the distance, the colorful sails of catamarans and sunfish vessels moved parallel with the horizon.

A lone swimmer was heading in, his powerful arms arcing out, then slicing back into the water with such perfect form that she wondered idly if he was training for something. She was a decent swimmer, but she'd always been fearful of swimming in the ocean.

Although, in light of the physical challenges she'd tackled in the last couple of days, a lap or two in the ocean didn't seem so intimidating. She made a thoughtful noise and smiled at the revelation.

The swimmer approached the shore, slowing as he reached shallow water. When he stood, her breath caught in her chest—it was Dominick. He'd spotted her and was walking toward her. He shook his head, sending water flying as more water sluiced off him, pulling on his dark swim trunks. The sight of his lean, muscular physique sent her vital signs into overdrive.

Winslow, too. As Dominick walked up on the beach, the dog was jumping up and down like a spring and barking like mad. She rattled his leash to shush him.

"I thought that was you," Dominick said, shaking his arms. "You're up early."

"I felt like taking a walk. The beach is so nice this time of day. Someone with my complexion can't afford to be out here when the sun is strong."

He gave her a thorough once-over. "You look like you've gotten some sun this week." Then he grinned. "Or at least a few more freckles."

"I have plenty of those," she agreed.

He grinned. "Careful, Vee. If I start thinking about all your freckles, I'll have to get back into that cold water."

She squirmed and looked away. He was teasing her. No man could find her speckled, white skin sexy. It made her feel even more ridiculous for having these feelings for him.

"Care if I walk back with you?" he asked.

"Not at all." Winslow growled, but she silenced him with a finger.

"Let me get my shirt and shoes." Dominick walked up into the dunes to retrieve a towel roll he'd stowed there. He dried off hurriedly, then leaned over and scooped up his shoes and jogged back to her. Violet noticed that every female head in the vicinity turned to watch him, and she felt a thrill that he was with her.

Well, not *with* her, really, but—

"Are you up to more research today?" he asked.

She wet her lips, ultra aware of how the last two days of "research" had ended. "What did you have in mind?"

"If we hurry, we can do a canopy climb. It's an all-day class because there's a bus ride involved, but it should be interesting."

"What's a canopy climb?"

"It's where you move through the tops of forests by a zip-line cable."

She angled her head. "Ever since I told you I was afraid of heights, you've had me dangling in the air."

He grinned. "Most extreme sports incorporate heights. Besides, you seem to be holding your own." He fell into step next to her. "Have you always been afraid of heights?"

"Ever since I was eleven."

"What happened when you were eleven?"

"I climbed a tree."

"And you couldn't get back down?"

She rubbed her lips together. "Actually, it was a tree I'd climbed lots of times, but my parents were leaving on a trip." She smiled. "I climbed it and pretended to be stuck, hoping my dad would forget about the trip and climb up to rescue me."

Dominick's mouth tightened. "But he didn't?"

She shook her head. "My parents left anyway, and then for some reason, I couldn't get down and my grandmother had to call the fire department. Ever since, I've had an aversion to heights."

"Understandable," he said, with a nod. "But there's one big difference now."

"What's that?"

He reached up and tugged on the end of her ponytail. "If you're stranded in a tree, I'll always come up to get you."

His eyes twinkled, but his voice was half-serious… or perhaps that was just wishful thinking on her part. Violet's chest suffused with emotion, entertaining the fantasy for a few seconds that she had the security of Dominick's big shoulder to lean on. When they returned to Atlanta, he'd be taking that sexy shoulder elsewhere, but while they were here…

"I'll go on the canopy climb," she said, letting out a deep breath. "If we can make arrangements for Winslow to stay at the spa."

Dominick grinned, then nodded to her feet. "We can, although I think he'd rather spend the day with you."

She looked down to see Winslow humping her leg. She reprimanded the dog and reached down to extricate him.

Dominick laughed then leaned close and murmured, "In the dog's defense, I know how he feels."

Violet blushed and tried to tamp down the excitement already building in her stomach. Her body knew how the day's activities would likely end…and every inch of her was looking forward to every inch of him.

14

DOMINICK CLICKED a carabiner from Violet's harness to a pulley on the metal zip line. They stood with a group of people on a platform high in a burgeoning tropical forest east of Miami. He wanted to kiss that worried look off her angelic face. Instead, he gave her hip a pat. "There. You're not going anywhere except where you want to go."

Beneath the helmet she wore, her eyes were wide. On this adventure, they wouldn't be hooked together.

He gave her a wink. "I'll always be a few feet behind you."

But guilt plucked at him. It was great to have the experience of three classes to get a better idea of how Sunpiper operated, but the whole research angle was wearing a little thin. He couldn't keep putting Violet in risky situations simply to get her worked up enough for him to swoop in and save the day with an amazing orgasm.

Then Violet gave him a tremulous smile that made his stomach clutch.

Or maybe he could, he thought crazily. Maybe he could buy the school and hire Violet to go on an extreme sports activity every day under the guise of business, and he could be there when she got home to relieve the tension in the most erotic ways.

Dominick winced and put a hand to his head. His mind was obviously still fuzzy after too many vodka tonics last night. Again. All he'd really wanted to do when they'd gotten back to the hotel was haul Violet into his bedroom for some thorough lovemaking.... But she'd written in her letter so disparagingly about having sex in bed that his ego wouldn't let him. He wanted her to remember their time together as exciting and thrilling, something that no other man would be able to top.

He exhaled as he clicked his own harness onto the zip line. Okay, it was conceited, but there it was. He didn't want another man to make love to Violet more...well.

But when the image of another man examining her freckles entered his mind, he frowned. He didn't like the idea of another man making love to Violet, period.

"Okay, here we go!" the instructor shouted. "Ease off the platform one at a time, leave several feet between you and the person in front of you."

When Violet's shoulders tensed, Dominick experienced a rush of protectiveness. He wanted to wrap his arms around her and make her feel safe.

Instead he leaned forward to whisper in her ear, "Just keep thinking what a good time we're going to have afterward."

Her lips parted in a gasp, but before she could respond, it was her turn to go. She bunched her body up and closed her eyes as she stepped off the platform. Dominick held his breath, poised to fling himself off the edge after her if by some fluke her equipment failed. When her weight settled safely on the cable, he released a sigh.

Her body froze and for a few seconds, she gripped the zip line with her gloved hands as if it were a lifeline. But when she realized she was stable on the line, she opened her eyes. Then, as the trainer had instructed, she leaned back and crossed her legs at the ankle, and began moving along the line on her pulley.

"Good girl," Dominick whispered, his chest filling with pride. She had guts.

When she had advanced along the cable far enough to put enough distance between them, Dominick grabbed on and swung down, enjoying the rush until his weight settled, then traveled after Vee.

The canopy tour was excellent. The instructor had done a good job on the bus ride over to educate the class about Florida's mandate to increase the state's tree foliage by twenty percent to combat global warming and to provide more habitat for threatened species. The guides who were spaced out among the students were also adept at pointing out sights along the way, both in the tree canopy and on the ground that changed from grassy to marshy. Chestnut-fronted macaws and white pelicans were plentiful, as well as migratory songbirds. Golden panthers sporting white chests were common in this area, both on the ground and in trees, but not at heights that endangered the people on the zip lines. When they traversed an area where three alligators were sunning themselves beside a brackish pool, Violet turned back to look at him over her shoulder, her eyes wide.

He gave her a comforting smile, troubled by how much he wanted her not just to be safe, but to enjoy herself. He'd been doing extreme sports for so long—jumping off mountains and going faster than a human being was meant to—he'd forgotten the simple enjoyment of a more tame experience, like this one. Seeing adventures through Violet's eyes had been a good lesson for him too, a reminder that even in extreme sports, there was room for all levels of daring and expertise.

And the accomplishment of mastering a feat wasn't as important if a person didn't enjoy the process. The fantastic sex notwithstanding, he'd had more fun with Violet these past couple of days than he'd had in…

A long damn time.

That strange feeling reminiscent of indigestion burned inside his chest again, and lingered until after the two-hour tour ended and they were back on terra firma.

"What did you think?" Dominick asked.

Violet's cheeks were pink with sun and excitement, her aqua-colored eyes bright. "It was fun!" She laughed. "My arms are tired and my legs are a little shaky, but I think I'll live."

She had a smudge on her chin and her ponytail sagged, with tendrils of red-gold hair pressed to her moist temples. Dominick thought she was the most beautiful woman he'd ever seen. "Good," he managed to say, rubbing at his breastbone.

She noticed his movement. "Are you okay?"

"Yeah. Just…indigestion, I think. I'll be…fine."

She stepped closer. "Dominick, behind you is a guy wearing a yellow T-shirt. I noticed him when I was stowing my gear. His shirt says 'Cambrian.' Isn't that the name of the company interested in buying Sunpiper?"

The company mentioned in Vee's research packet. Dominick pursed his mouth and nodded. "Yeah." He turned and nonchalantly took in the man wearing the yellow T-shirt. The guy seemed to be conferring with another man, who was wearing glasses and designer "outdoorsy" clothing—the guy was a financial squint if he'd ever seen one.

He looked back to Violet. "Good eye, Vee. Looks like I'm going to have to make my move."

"So you're still interested in buying the school?"

He nodded. "Enough to set up an appointment to meet with the owners before I leave town."

She smiled, obviously pleased that she'd taken part in the "research" that had led to his decision. On his part, he was relieved that a legitimate business issue had emerged to justify what had been a flimsy excuse for a business trip.

Violet had the names of the owners stored in her PDA, so when they were let off at Sunpiper, Dominick asked the receptionist if they could make an appointment to see one or both men. He explained why, then handed over a business card. The woman checked with the owners' respective assistants and informed him that both men would be back in the office the day after Christmas. "How about first thing the morning of the twenty-sixth?"

"Sounds good," Dominick said. "Thank you."

As they left the building and climbed into his rented convertible, Violet was animated—and so, so sexy. "I can help you with any additional research between now and then. The local library might have—"

"Vee," he interrupted. "You don't have to be here for the meeting."

She blanched even whiter. "I didn't mean…that is, I didn't presume you would include me in the meeting."

"That's not what I meant." He hesitated, hating to give her an opening to leave, but knowing it was the right thing to do. "I was thinking that if you wanted to go back to spend Christmas Eve with your folks, you still can. I'll fly you back myself, in fact. It was selfish of me to take you away from your family simply because I don't have much use for the holiday."

She was quiet for several long seconds, staring at her hands. "Thank you for the offer, but that won't be necessary. My parents aren't home."

"Did they make plans to go out of town after you told them about the business trip?"

She shook her head. "They had an opportunity to go on a cruise to Panama with some new friends and asked if I cared if we skipped Christmas." She looked up and tried to smile, but failed miserably. "It was an all expenses paid trip—it would've been silly for them to pass it up."

Dominick's heart squeezed. Her parents had dumped her on her first Christmas without her grandparents? Damn, that was cold. A fierce sensation of protectiveness welled in his chest. He wanted to pull her into his arms and offer his shoulder for her to cry on, but that seemed a little too…personal.

But he had other means of offering comfort.

Dominick reached over to cover Vee's hand. "Their loss and my gain. Without you, I wouldn't be sitting here contemplating buying this sports school and expanding my business."

She nodded and almost smiled this time.

An overwhelming urge to make her happy plowed through him. He couldn't offer anything in terms of a relationship, but he could fulfill the fantasies she'd written about in the letter to herself.

"In fact…" He picked up her hand and kissed her palm. "I think we should go back to the hotel and celebrate our successful research trip."

VIOLET'S ARM TINGLED from Dominick's kiss. Her libido was so worked up from the day's activities, something from his direction as subtle as an eye twitch would have had the same effect.

But she appreciated the effort.

And she was grateful that he hadn't quizzed her about her parents' casual dismissal. It was embarrassing enough to admit it without belaboring the point. And the distraction he was offering…

She wanted to be wanted, needed to be needed. When she was with Dominick, she felt alive and special. He had a way of pulling her out of herself…. With this man she could be bold.

She smiled in response. "Hurry."

He broke every speed limit getting them back to the hotel, then tossed the keys to a valet driver. They hurried through the lobby like horny teenagers, then rode up in the glass elevator, which only kicked her pulse higher.

Dusk was setting when they burst into the suite. He was kissing her before the door closed. The thought of taking a shower flitted through her mind, but she discarded it as being too…romantic. The only thing that was keeping her from falling head over heels in love with this man was the fact that the sex was fast and raw. She could pretend it meant as little to her as it did to him.

They left a trail of shoes and clothes from the door, down the stairs and into the sitting area. When she realized that he was leading her out onto the balcony, her heart raced wildly. He unlocked the sliding door and pushed it open, then backed outside and pulled her along with him. She wore only her underwear—black panties and a black underwire athletic bra. The wind swirled around her as if to remind her that at this height, she was susceptible to being plucked up and blown away. Her leg muscles contracted to ground her to the gritty tile floor beneath her feet.

"I got you," he murmured.

She clung to him and forced herself to look.

The sun was setting, leaving behind just enough radiance to light the clouds hovering on the horizon, casting a teal-colored glow over the water and the sand.

She sighed, overcome by the majestic scene— before her and next to her. Dominick was barefoot, and naked from the waist up. His muscular shoulders and powerful chest gave way to a flat stomach. His gray-colored khaki pants hung low on his lean hips, revealing the waistband of his boxers. His dark hair was being tousled by the wind, falling over his forehead. When he lowered his gaze to hers, his blue eyes reflected the hunger pulsing through her body.

He turned her until her back pressed against the railing. Then he removed the clasp from her hair and the wind picked up the ends. The emptiness of space around her shoulders and neck made her stomach flutter.

"It's okay," he murmured against her ear. "Did you know that we're all born with the fear of falling?"

She shook her head.

"Go with it," he said. "Use it. Feel how good the air is on your body." He reached around and un-hooked her bra. Her breasts fell free and the tips instantly grew hard when the wind kissed them. She arched into him and back over the railing as his warm mouth closed over a nipple. When starbursts of sensations reverberated through her body, she cried out, but the noise was carried away on the breeze.

He laved both breasts and rolled her panties down to her knees. She pulled at the waistband of his pants, unfastening the fly and releasing his thick erection into her hand. Dominick moaned and surged against her palm, then fumbled in his pocket for his wallet and a condom. He rolled it on quickly, then turned her around to face the railing. He bent over her, bracing his arms on either side of hers.

The ground tilted, falling away some thirty stories below.

"I got you, Vee," he murmured in her ear. His chest was warm on her back, his chin tucked into the curve of her neck. He pushed his cock into her from behind, an inch, then two inches. She contracted around him, trying to pull him deeper inside, but he resisted. Then he reached around with one hand to find her clit and matched a slow circular rhythm with his thrusts.

The sensation was beyond incredible. Between Dominick and their breezy, sky-high backdrop, her body was being stroked inside and out. The climax sleeping in her belly for most of the day, nudged by looks and touches from Dominick as they rode through the treetops, roared awake and began to engulf her body. Responding to her moans, Dominick thrust deep inside her. Violet's head spun from the sensory overload. And when the orgasm claimed her, her legs threatened to give way. She felt as if she were falling...tumbling over and over on the wind...

Dominick surrendered to his climax scarce heartbeats later, his body contracting around hers. He groaned her name as he drove into her, deeper and deeper, until his shudders slowed, then ceased.

When Violet opened her eyes, moist blue-black air enveloped her. The light on the horizon had all but slipped away, but lights on the ground far below twinkled. A long line of tiki torches had been lit on the beach, perhaps to commemorate the holidays.

She remained still, astonished by her body's intense response to his. Her limbs sang with exhaustion. He pulled her hair away from her neck and left a kiss there. She closed her eyes briefly, wanting to buy into the fantasy that they could continue like this.

When he stood, the wind cooled her skin where their bodies had worked up a sweat. He pulled away from her gently, then turned her around in his arms.

"That was pretty great," he said, his voice low and raspy. His breathing hadn't yet returned to normal.

"Yes," she murmured in agreement.

"I'm starving. Let's go get something to eat."

She wanted to go…she wanted to prolong the fantasy of being Dominick's girlfriend, but in her mind she fast-forwarded to the place where the relationship would inevitably blow apart.

"I don't think so," she said. "I need to pick up Winslow, and I'd like to make some phone calls."

"Oh." He scratched the back of his neck. "Okay. I guess I thought…"

She leaned over to roll up her panties. She couldn't find her bra in the darkness and decided to look for it later. She straightened. "Thought what?"

He hesitated, then shook his head. "Never mind."

Violet strode past him and stepped back into the

room. Better to act aloof, especially now. Because earlier, when she'd experienced the sensation of falling, it had nothing to do with falling over the edge of the balcony...but everything to do with falling in love with Dominick.

15

Christmas Eve

VIOLET HAD ENTERTAINED fantasies about being licked
awake, but the reality didn't quite live up to the
dream—especially since her early-morning admirer
had big eyes and an underbite.

"Good morning, Winslow." She stroked his head
and smiled at the clear, bright sun shining through the
window of her bedroom. Suddenly, she realized what
day it was. "It's Christmas Eve!" she exclaimed,
bounding out of bed.

Picking up on her excitement, Winslow jumped
down and followed her to the window, barking.

"Shh! You might wake Dominick. He was probably out late again last night."

At the mention of Dominick's name, the dog
growled.

She pointed her finger. "No growling." Then
Violet sighed and crouched to pick up the dog,

cradling him against her chest. "Besides," she whispered, "I think I love him."

Winslow angled his hairy head at her.

"I know. It's crazy and it's going nowhere. But it's wonderful to be in love for Christmas. It's like a gift I wasn't expecting." She pushed her nose against the dog's cold little snout. "And you can't tell anyone."

He whined.

Violet smiled and used one hand to slide open the window. The sounds of the ocean and gulls rushed in to envelop her. The view stretched before her like a postcard—azure water, majestic palm trees, turquoise sky, winding beach. It wasn't the snow she'd hoped to see for Christmas, but if she squinted, the white sand was a passable facsimile.

At least she wouldn't be alone for Christmas.

She set Winslow on the floor, wincing at her sore muscles but conceding that she'd put her body through a lot in the past few days. The jumping, the climbing, the swinging...

And the sex.

She picked up a pillow from the bed and hugged it to her chest. Being with Dominick was so exhilarating, so exciting that just thinking about having his body inside hers sent chills over her skin.

So this was what Dr. Alexander had meant when she'd explained to her students the delights of intense sexual chemistry. Dominick made her feel as if she were going to fly apart from sheer pleasure, and it wasn't just the sex—it was the time and the place and the passion. The Sex for Beginners class had given her a peek into an erotic world, but Dominick had allowed her to experience it.

In hindsight, it wasn't surprising that sex with Dominick would be electrifying—the man, after all, had constructed a business around his hobby of extreme sports. It only made sense that all his physical pursuits would be just as zealous.

Violet sighed. No wonder women were crazy for the man. He was handsome, sexy, successful, fun-loving and always on the hunt for a new challenge. But she could also see how his short attention span could spell disaster for anyone in a relationship with him. Inevitably, he would move on when something more interesting came along.

She put the pillow back on the bed and fluffed it idly. That was why she had to keep her feelings for Dominick to herself. When they returned to Atlanta and went their separate ways, no one would know what had transpired in Miami. She would simply be one of dozens of women who had fallen under his spell and lived to dream about it.

She dressed quickly, donning another black suit and one of the sleeveless blouses that Lillian had loaned her. She didn't know how she and Dominick were going to spend the day, but she thought it best to dress for business. It seemed likely they wouldn't be taking any more extreme sports classes.

Which probably meant no more sex, she realized, since they wouldn't be rubbing against each other all day.

She frowned into the mirror and gave her ponytail an extra yank to make it even tighter.

When she slipped from her bedroom with Winslow trotting at her feet, she was surprised to see the sliding glass door to the balcony standing open. Dominick sat outside, reading the newspaper and sipping a cup of coffee, looking fit and relaxed in shorts and a T-shirt. He looked up and smiled, then waved.

Her heart expanded and she chastised herself— she couldn't go around with her newfound feelings for him written all over her face. She didn't want to put Dominick in an awkward situation, and she could do without the humiliation of rejection, especially on the heels of her parents' abandonment. She'd gotten more from this trip than she'd ever expected and she was grateful for the memories that would last a lifetime.

It would have to be enough.

She schooled her face into a nonchalant expression and walked over to the open doorway, struck anew by the memory of what had transpired there last night. Her throat tightened and her breasts tingled. In the daylight, the railing looked innocuous, not at all like a prop for a session of earth-shattering sex.

"Good morning," Dominick said cheerfully.

Standing next to her, Winslow bared his teeth and growled.

"Good morning," she murmured, then chastised the dog.

He nodded to a carafe on the table next to his chair. "Want coffee?"

"Sure." She reached for the empty cup he'd set out, but next to it, neatly folded, was the bra she'd been wearing last night, the one she couldn't find…afterward. Her face flamed as she discreetly stuffed it in her jacket pocket. She was like Dr. Jekyll and Mr. Hyde— by day she was uptight and proper, but in Dominick's arms, she became a wild sex kitten. A breeze picked up and she was suddenly reminded how high they were. Feeling overwhelmed by the physical and emotional onslaught, she took a step backward, flailing for the stability of the door frame. Dominick looked up, his face creased in concern, and stood to steady her.

"Are you okay, Vee?"

But his touch only increased her distress. She gave a nervous little laugh and pulled away. "On second thought, I think I'll take Winslow for a walk." She turned and went back inside, breathing deeply to calm her nerves.

Dominick followed her, juggling his paper and the coffee as he closed the sliding door behind him. "Do you want to get some breakfast?"

She wanted to go with him. If he'd made eye contact with her, had asked the question in a way or a tone that made it seem as if he cared, she would've joined him. Instead, his voice was casual and his gaze elsewhere, and she knew he was only asking to be polite.

"Thank you, but I think I'll pass," she murmured, thinking she could use the walk to start weaning her body and her heart away from Dominick. He'd brought her here to do a job, after all. "What's on the agenda today?"

He smiled. "It's Christmas Eve, you know."

She nodded, her chest constricting.

"So, I thought we might do something…Christmasy."

She arched an eyebrow. "Like what?"

He extended the newspaper to her. "Like this."

She glanced at the story headline—Local Charity Asks for Help Delivering Christmas Cheer to Kids.

"They need toys," he said, looking almost sheepish. "And I was hoping you'd help me shop."

Her heart unfurled with warmth and something else—hope. Perhaps Dominick Burns wasn't the shallow, narcissistic playboy that everyone made him out to be. She blinked back sudden moisture before she made an idiot of herself for being so tender-hearted. "I think that's a wonderful gesture, Dominick, and I'd be happy to help you."

He grinned. "Good. There's a mall nearby with a big toy store."

She bit her lip. "Can we take Winslow?"

He glanced down at the dog standing between them. "Sure, it's Christmas." He reached down to pet the dog's head, but Winslow snapped at him. Dominick jerked back and frowned. "When you're finished walking Mr. Sunshine, stop by the café and we'll leave from there."

VIOLET SMILED AS she watched Dominick show a group of kids how to balance on a skateboard. It hadn't taken him long to draw a crowd, and the kids watched him in rapt attention. He extolled the virtues of outdoor sports, then thrilled everyone—clerks included—when he announced that every kid in the store could have their pick of skates, stand-up scooter, or skateboard.

Her heart expanded as she watched him. Dominick looked like a big kid himself as he played all the interactive games in the store, tossed sponge footballs and exclaimed over some toy he'd had when he was a kid. She had explained the reason for their trip to an attentive salesclerk, who spoke to the manager and offered to deliver any toys that Dominick purchased to the charity.

"Isn't this place great?" Dominick asked her, his arms wide. "Let's start shopping, Vee."

"Do you have a budget?" she asked, ever conscientious about spending someone else's money.

He sobered slightly, then tugged on her ponytail. "Not when it's for something so special." He picked a doggie chew toy from a nearby shelf and offered it to Winslow. The Pekingese sniffed the toy suspiciously, then took it into his mouth.

It was a side of Dominick Violet had never seen before. In that moment, she loved him so much, her chest hurt.

DOMINICK FELT ridiculously pleased when the ugly little dog took the chew toy without snapping his hand off. But it was nothing compared to the feeling that swelled in his chest when he looked at Vee. Over the year that she'd worked for him, he'd learned to trust her judgment and her integrity. But since arriving in Miami, he'd seen a different side of her—a sexy, daring side.

Together, it was a powerful package.

They walked around the store and, using the needs spelled out in the newspaper article as her guide, she pointed out age-appropriate gifts, working out quantity details with the salesclerk. Dolls, trucks, books and games of every sort were removed from shelves and stacked into carts as they went along. Violet handled everything methodically and efficiently, with a warmth and sense of kindness that, strangely, fueled his lust for her even higher.

And when an alien voice in his head whispered that perhaps what he felt for her was more than lust, he dismissed it as holiday sentimentality.

And later, when they left the store and Violet took the time to have Winslow's picture taken with Santa and Dominick experienced that recurring pressure in his chest, he dismissed it as holiday sentimentality.

And finally, when they discovered a temporary ice skating rink that had been set up indoors for Christmas and she turned a glorious smile his way, Dominick rubbed his breastbone and started thinking he was experiencing a cardiac incident.

"Let's go skating!" she cried.

He balked. "Um…I don't know how."

Her eyes widened, then she grinned. "I'll teach you."

He started to protest. The idea of hobbling around on blades, losing his balance and landing on his backside on a sheet of cold, hard ice didn't rank high on his life list. Doing all of those things in front of Violet held even less appeal.

But her eyes were so big and luminous, how could he refuse her? Besides, she had learned to bungee jump, paraglide and ride on a zip line, all at his urging, so he owed her one.

At least one.

"Okay," he said, relenting. They rented skates and fastened Winslow's leash to the outer railing. Then she gave him a minilesson, teaching him how to balance, how to start out by walking on the ice to get the feel of it.

"Lean on your left foot, then push out diagonally with your right foot." She demonstrated, making it seem easy as she glided along, looking impossibly sexy in her prim black suit and white ice skates. She was an enigma, this naive young woman in a grown-up body, so mature in some ways, so innocent in other ways.

She laughed and skated circles around him, obviously delighting in his awkward antics. He leaned forward, then backward, then flailed like a windmill before falling spectacularly and landing on his back.

Her lovely face appeared over his, her ponytail hanging down. "Are you okay?"

He nodded. "But I'd rather jump out of a plane."

She laughed and put out her arm to help him to his feet. He was surprised that she could counter his weight and still maintain her balance. Once he was stabilized, she stood in front of him and held his hands, then began to skate backward slowly, pulling him along.

"Bend your knees," she said. "Relax."

"I'm trying," he said, thinking that her hands were as soft as the cashmere robe he'd bought the other day. "Where did you learn to skate?"

"My grandfather taught me. He grew up in Wisconsin, so he skated and played hockey." She smiled. "He was pretty good."

Her cheeks were pink from the exertion, her freckles prominent. "So are you," he said.

She shook her head. "Not really. But my grandfather always took me skating at Christmastime."

He smiled. "So tell me about this magical Christmas you always dreamed of."

"We'd have a tree with lots of ornaments, carols, gifts and…snow."

He raised his eyebrows. "In Atlanta?"

She shrugged. "A girl can dream."

Violet had a fanciful imagination, but she seemed to keep a lid on her dreams. Maybe because she'd always been disappointed?

"I'll let you in on a secret," he murmured.

"What?"

"Santa's bringing you a gift."

"Oh, you have a direct line to Santa?"

He grinned. "I'm his secret shopper."

Her eyebrows went up. "You don't shop, not even for your girlfriends," she protested. Then she blanched. "I mean…I wasn't implying…that I'm your girlfriend. I meant the other women in your…life."

Dominick fought a belly laugh, watching Vee squirm over semantics. "Just for the record, I don't have a girlfriend. And you're right—I don't shop… usually. But I made an exception for you."

Her eyes lit with interest before she turned wary. "What is it?"

"I can't tell you," he said, feeling mischievous. "And no peeking."

"Okay," she said with a sigh. "In that case…"

She let go of his hands. He reached for her, but she skated away from him, in front of him, doing little turns and maneuvers that always kept her just out of reach. It gave him a taste of what it was like not to have Violet…and it left him feeling empty.

He lost his balance and landed smack on his back again. He lay there and groaned, but the hard landing must have knocked some sense into him, because he decided one thing: despite what Vee had written in that letter about boring places to have sex, the one thing he didn't want empty tonight was his bed.

_16_

VIOLET COULDN'T HAVE imagined a more wondrous Christmas Eve—watching Dominick buying all those toys, knowing that so many underprivileged children would wake up with something special tomorrow morning, going ice skating and laughing at his good-natured attempts to learn, then sharing a romantic meal together. Even Winslow had warmed toward Dominick, lying with his head on Dominick's foot during dinner at an outside café.

Her feelings toward Dominick were running full tilt. Everything he did, everything he said, reinforced her desire to be with him. And after today, after the way he'd looked into her eyes, she was even starting to think…starting to hope…

Well, a girl could dream, couldn't she?

He said he didn't have a girlfriend. And he'd bought her a Christmas gift, after all—which was more than her parents had done.

When they returned to the hotel suite, her mood was buoyant and her heart was pounding. When the door closed behind them, Dominick kissed her in the entryway, a thorough exploration of her mouth that took her breath away. Then he cupped her face.

"Stay with me tonight, Vee."

In his room…in his bed. She knew if she did, she wouldn't be able to hide her feelings for him afterward, wouldn't be able to pretend that she was cool with a sex-only relationship, with an occasional booty-call.

But she didn't want to spend the rest of her life kicking herself for not jumping at this opportunity to find a way out of herself, no matter how remote the possibility that Dominick felt the same way about her. And she didn't want to wake up Christmas morning all alone.

She nodded against his hand, and was rewarded by the desire that flared in his eyes. When Winslow barked at their feet to remind them of his presence, she excused herself to settle him into her room. Once there, Violet stared at herself in the mirror, marveling at how much she'd changed since she'd arrived in Miami. And it was all because of Dominick.

In hindsight, maybe underneath the relentless teasing, maybe he'd been attracted to her all along, just as she'd been holding a torch for him. Why else would he have invited her to Miami for Christmas instead of one of his women friends? He might have hoped that she'd sleep with him, but he couldn't have known for sure. The other girls would've been safer bets. And any of them would've been more gung ho about the extreme sports classes than she'd been.

Violet pulled out a turquoise-colored silk teddy and black panties from the handful of lingerie that she'd grabbed before she'd left, then released her ponytail and arranged her hair around her shoulders. Violet nodded at her reflection. Yes, Dominick had to have feelings for her. She couldn't have misread his cues all day…all week…

Violet smiled. "Merry Christmas to me," she whispered.

She checked on Winslow and found him snoring on her bed. Then she padded across the living room and knocked on Dominick's bedroom door, her pulse skipping. She ached for him, but she hadn't experienced an adrenaline rush all day—would the sex be different this time? Less exciting?

When he answered the door wearing only pale-colored boxers, her heartbeat went into the stratosphere.

His gaze swept her from head to toe. "Vee, you look…"

"Different?" she asked, lifting her chin.

"Amazing," he corrected, then kissed her and pulled her inside, his strong hands roving down her back. She wondered if the day would ever come that she'd want him to take it slow. Right now all she wanted was him inside her, as soon as possible.

Dominick closed the door and handed her a drink. "Cheers," he said, his eyes twinkling as he held up his glass.

"Merry Christmas," she murmured, clinking her glass to his. She sipped the drink, then smiled happily. "Love in an Elevator."

"I thought you liked it on the plane."

"I did, thanks." She glanced all around his room, keeping an eye out for any bags or packages that would give her a clue as to what he might have gotten her. No grown woman should be so excited about a Christmas gift, but she couldn't help it. Would this be the first of many gifts he'd get her? The first of many Christmases they would spend together?

Dominick clasped her hand and led her to sit on the edge of the king-size bed. Then he set their drinks on the nightstand and turned his attention back to her. He knelt on the floor in front of her, kissing her while he slid his hands up her thighs and lifted the teddy up and off. He stared at her for a few seconds and she felt herself bloom under his gaze.

He lowered his head and feasted on her breasts like a starved man, laving and drawing on the nipples until they were hard little knots. He reached down to remove her panties, and she knew the second he realized they were crotchless. His hands stopped and his breathing escalated to a moan. Then he eased her back on the bed and before she could exhale, he had parted her knees and his mouth was on her.

Violet had heard about oral sex, had read about it, had taken quizzes in *Cosmo* about it, had even tried it on a guy once, but no one had ever returned the favor. The sheer shock of the sensations splintering through her body nearly sent her off the bed. He gave her a long, slow tongue-lashing, then he latched onto her clit and sipped at her wetness. She cried out and pulled at his hair, wanting him to stop, but not about to let him until she'd experienced it to the end.

But the end came sooner than she expected. It was his skilled tongue, she thought wildly as an orgasm erupted in her belly like a fireball. She squeezed his shoulders with her knees as the pleasure burned through her body.

"Dominick…please…oh, yes…Dominick." The torture was so exquisite she didn't have words to describe it. She had barely begun to recover when he stood and fumbled for a condom on the nightstand. He quickly sheathed himself, then pulled her ankles to his shoulders and thrust into her with a groan. His face was contorted with a mix of pleasure and pain, and he appeared to be restraining himself.

But Violet wanted all of him—now.

"You feel so good inside me," she said, contracting around him. "Fill me up, Dominick…harder… faster."

He looked down at her with hooded eyes. A muscle in his jaw worked. He kissed her ankle, then bit down gently as his body began to shudder against hers. "Ahh…ahh…ahh." He came and came, seemingly against his will, then collapsed forward onto the bed.

Violet curled up next to Dominick, utterly sated. Their chemistry was so amazing, it was as if he knew exactly what to do to make her lose her inhibitions. He wrapped his arms around her and kissed her hair. New, wondrous love flowered in her heart. She never wanted this night to end.

She gave in to peaceful dreams in his arms and jarred awake around five in the morning.

Christmas morning, she realized. She sat up, troubled to find Dominick gone until she heard the sound of the shower running in his bathroom. The room was warm, she conceded. Since her body was covered with a sheen of perspiration, he was probably trying to cool off. She turned on a light and adjusted the thermostat, then considered joining Dominick in the shower. Why not? She was a different person now, the sensual, confident woman she'd always wanted to be.

Then a mischievous thought slipped into her mind—the gift Dominick had bought her. She was dying to know what it was and if it would give her a clue as to how he felt about her.

She bit into her lip. The old Violet would never peek….

But the new Violet might.

Wouldn't it be better if she knew what it was so that when he gave it to her, her response would be appropriate? It could save them both from embarrassed or hurt feelings if, for example, he'd bought her a souvenir snow globe or something gadgety, versus something romantic.

It was already Christmas morning, she reasoned. He'd be giving it to her soon anyway. She pulled on her teddy and glanced around the room. Where would Dominick hide a gift?

She knelt to look under the bed, but it was a pedestal model with no space underneath. Next she quietly opened the closet. His clothes hung neatly from hangers, some of them still covered by dry cleaner's bags—clothes that she'd probably picked up, she thought wryly—but no shopping bags.

Then she spied the dresser drawers. Three of them. She walked over and slid open the first one—folded T-shirts and shorts. Then she slid out the second one—his toiletry bag. Then she slid open the bottom drawer and her pulse blipped. Amongst his socks and underwear was a gift bag.

She reached for the bag, but then was distracted when something else caught her eye. Something pink. Violet frowned and a memory chord strummed even before she could fully process what she was seeing.

A pink polka-dotted envelope.

17

Violet stared at the pink polka-dotted envelope she thought had been discarded.

She pulled it out of Dominick's dresser drawer, her mind reeling in confusion as she turned it over in her hands. Why on earth would Dominick have her letter?

And then the contents landed on her like a bomb.

Her letter of sexual fantasies.

About not being impressed with sex.

About hoping someday to experience exciting sex.

She covered her mouth with her hand to stifle a cry. When she looked up, Dominick was coming out of the bathroom with a towel wrapped around his waist.

"I didn't mean to wake you, Vee. I was coming back—"

"Where did you get this?" Violet asked, holding up the envelope with a shaking hand.

Dominick's mouth opened, then closed. He gestured to the letter, then put his hands on his hips, obviously at a loss.

"Answer me," Violet said, breathing hard.

He closed his eyes briefly. "It was…in the envelope of research you sent to my house."

Her mind spooled back over that day. She had received the letter, had read it, then had stuffed it under something on her desk when Lillian had come into her office. Later she had done the research for Dominick, and put together the packet to have couriered to his house. She must have inadvertently included the letter with the other papers from her desk.

"This letter is *private*," she said in a strangled voice.

"I know." He took a step toward her. "I…I'm sorry, Vee."

She put up her hands. "*Don't* call me that," she said, backing up. "Why do you still have it?"

"I…didn't know how to return it without embarrassing you. And it seemed wrong to throw it away."

Realization dawned on her—the last-minute invitation to Miami, the sex…the *exciting* sex. Mortification bled through her. "You planned this entire trip because of this letter, didn't you?"

He didn't have to respond, she could see the answer on his face. His primary conquest hadn't been Sunpiper—it had been her.

"You wanted to what—prove that you could seduce me? Show the ingénue what she's missing?" She choked on a sob. "Make me fall in love with you?"

His face had gone dark, but he remained silent.

"Did you have a big laugh about it with your friends?" she asked, crying now.

"No," he said finally, his voice low. "No else knows about the letter."

She wiped at her eyes. "So I was just your personal project for the holidays?"

He didn't respond, which only made the hole in her heart bigger.

"I'm leaving," she said, backing out of the room.

"Vee—Violet, wait. Let me explain."

She stopped and waited…and waited…

DOMINICK WANTED to put his arms around Violet and admit he was a jerk, to say how sorry he was, but he had no defense. He *had* planned the trip for his own amusement, intrigued by the prospect of bedding Violet and introducing her to thrilling sex. He hadn't considered how condescending she would find it because he'd never dreamed that she'd find the letter.

And he hadn't counted on the fact that she would turn the tables on him, make him so horny he could barely perform without embarrassing himself…and in between, be so sweet and sincere and fun that he'd come dangerously close to falling in love with her.

He couldn't tell her all of those things, because she would never believe him now. And it was his own damn fault.

"I'll get dressed and fly you home," he said thickly.

She made a disgusted noise. "You can't be serious," she said, her expression filled with loathing. "I don't want to spend another second with you. I'll find my own way home."

18

VIOLET WALKED BLINDLY to her bedroom, her vision hindered by tears. Winslow was scratching at the door, so she assumed they'd woken him up with their loud exchange. When she opened the door, he danced backward, whining, as if he could sense her mood.

She took a two-minute shower and dressed as quickly as she could, still crying. She yanked her hair back into a ponytail and brushed on powder to try to conceal some of the redness, but it was useless—she looked like redheaded zombie.

The damnable letter went into the bottom of her purse. She tossed her clothes and shoes into her suitcase, uncaring of their disarray. Then she shepherded Winslow back into his carrier under protest, kicked open the bedroom door and carried him out with her suitcase.

Dominick stood near the door to his bedroom, fully dressed. She could barely look at him. She was so humiliated…especially for the feelings she'd developed for him. She had been falling in love with him and all the while, he'd been laughing at her, pitying her loveless life. Waves of shame washed over her.

And she had the worst case of hiccups from her crying jag.

When Dominick made a move to help with her luggage, she stiffened and pulled away. But by the time she came out of the bedroom with her second load, he had carried her suitcase and Winslow out into the hall.

"I don't want your help," she declared, daring him to defy her.

He looked as if he wanted to say something, but instead, he nodded and set the bags down.

"Goodbye, Dominick," she said pointedly, and pulled the door closed in his face. She wrestled everything onto a shoulder or arm and managed to get it all to the freight elevator. She knew she looked like a bag lady walking through the hotel lobby. A bellman stopped to assist her and she asked if he could hail her a cab.

Violet kept the fresh tears at bay until she'd settled into the cab and they'd pulled away from the curb headed toward the Miami airport. Then she pulled the pink polka-dot envelope from her purse and scanned the letter. She burst into tears again when she realized it truly was as embarrassing as she remembered. The thought of Dominick reading the letter and using it to entertain himself made her throb with humiliation. No wonder he'd known all the right buttons to push. The letter was practically a how-to guide for turning her on.

God, his betrayal just hurt so much.

She blew her nose and tried to stop the little mewling noises coming from her throat, but she couldn't help it. The cabbie kept sending her worried looks, and Winslow pawed at the carrier door. It didn't help that outside, jagged lines of lightning lit the humid early morning sky. She tried to soothe the little dog with comforting words.

"We should've stayed home, Winslow." Which didn't exactly soothe *her.*

At the airport, the driver helped to carry her luggage to the curb, then accepted the tip with a nod.

"Merry Christmas, ma'am."

Violet tried her best to smile. "Merry Christmas to you, too."

As she turned away, she let out a long breath. So much for her magical Christmas. No one wanted her.

Initially, she'd been worried that not many flights would be running Christmas day. But the airport was packed. Who knew it was such a busy travel day? Thank goodness Winslow's carrier was small enough to carry on board. But the real problem, she discovered when she tried to secure a seat back to Atlanta, were the thunderstorms that had developed across the southeast.

"Listen for announcements," the attendant told her with the quick smile of a harried person. "But between you and me, it looks like nothing's moving in or out of here for at least a couple of hours."

To think that she'd hoped for snow for Christmas, and here she was stranded at the Miami airport.

"Is there anything else I can do for you, ma'am?"

Violet swallowed her bitter disappointment. "Would you happen to have a paper shredder back there?"

"Yes, ma'am."

She dug out her the polka-dot envelope containing the damnable letter. "Will it handle this?"

"Yes, ma'm."

Violet handed over the envelope and stood there while the woman fed the letter through, creating pink confetti on the other side.

Good riddance, she thought.

If not for that stupid letter, she might not have let herself be convinced that her life was boring. If not for that stupid letter, she wouldn't have considered Dominick's illicit invitation. If not for that stupid letter, she wouldn't have had sex with Dominick on a counter…in an open field…on a penthouse balcony… in his bed—

"Ma'am?" the representative asked. "Are you okay?"

"I'm fine," Violet said. "Could you direct me to the animal relief areas?"

"Stay on this floor, down this corridor, look for the signs."

"May I take him out of his carrier?"

"As long as he's housebroken and leashed."

"Thank you." She picked up Winslow's carrier and moved to a public seating area where she could hear P.A. announcements and have proximity to the exit door that led to a patch of grass where she could walk Winslow if necessary. She let him out of the carrier, and since there were several empty chairs, she let him climb up on the seat next to her where he curled up and gnawed on the chew toy that Dominick had given him.

Violet's mind wouldn't shut down, wouldn't stop torturing her with images of what she'd experienced with Dominick. The man had missed his calling as an actor. *She'd* certainly been fooled by his warm eyes, easy laugh and charitable contributions. She'd actually begun to think there was more to him than met the eye.

And what met the eye was so mouth-watering.

She rubbed her throbbing temples. In fact, everything inside her hurt. Every breath delivered new currents of pain. After she returned to Atlanta, hopefully her frantic daily routine would help her to keep going, to put this ugly chapter of her life behind her. Work had always been her salvation…and it would be again.

Christmas tunes played over the P.A. system. "I'll

Be Home for Christmas" was playing, the Bing Crosby version. The words made Violet's eyes water. If the weather broke, she *would* be home for Christmas. Too bad no one else would be there.

She unzipped her bulging suitcase since she had time to rearrange things. When she opened it, she was shocked to find the gift bag she'd seen in Dominick's dresser drawer. She frowned, wondering when he'd—

When he'd moved her suitcase to the hallway. He must have stuck it inside.

She pursed her mouth. He had a lot of nerve, forcing his Christmas gift on her after what he'd done. Violet shook the bag. Whatever it was, she was going to get rid of it.

She bit into her lip and looked at Winslow. "Should I open it?"

He dropped the chew toy and barked enthusiastically.

"Maybe it's something else you can chew on," Violet said dryly. She sighed and conceded that her curiosity was burning. Besides, she wanted to know what it was, just so she could hate it. Opening the gift bag, she reached inside and withdrew a box…and gasped.

It was the vintage Little People doll, the one she'd seen in the boutique, the one that hadn't been for sale. Her throat tightened. Dominick must have paid a hefty sum to convince the owner to part with it. His comment yesterday about having a spending budget came back to her.

Not when it's for something so special.

No matter how she tried, she couldn't hate it. She'd simply have to find a way to reimburse Dominick for the doll.

Which was going to be hard, she acknowledged, since she'd also just lost her best client.

When she slid the box back into the bag, she noticed a small envelope with "Vee" written on it in Dominick's bold handwriting. She pressed her lips together, telling herself she didn't care about anything he had to say.

Then she glanced at the doll. He'd bought it before their confrontation this morning. That had to mean something didn't it? Then she released a dry laugh.

Maybe that he was feeling guilty, the jerk.

She pressed her lips together, then slid her thumb under the flap of the envelope. It was a simple white Christmas card with a dove on the front—almost… romantic.

Vee, it isn't world peace, but I hope this gift makes you smile. Dominick

Her vision blurred. She had to hand it to him— the man was smooth. She could almost believe he was sincere. Just like when they were taking the classes…having sex…ice-skating. Miserable tears fell down her cheeks. Winslow whined, then licked her face, the dear dog.

"Maybe Patricia will let me adopt you when we get home," Violet murmured. "Would you like that?"

She smiled, realizing it was nearly impossible to be sad when a dog was licking your face.

"Look," someone yelled. "It's snowing!"

Violet lifted her head and gasped. Sure enough, outside the window white flakes were falling fast enough to accumulate on the grass. It was over eighty degrees outside—how was it possible? She stood and went to the window, pressing her nose against it, awestruck. All around her, people exclaimed in wonder.

At the sound of a commotion in the corridor, Violet turned, then sucked in a sharp, painful breath. Dominick was striding toward her carrying a…decorated Christmas tree?

He had an entourage of people with him, some dressed as elves who were passing out gifts, some dressed as carolers who were serenading the crowd. Violet's mind spun in bewilderment.

He stopped an arm's length in front of her, then planted the tree on the floor.

Her heart was thudding in her chest. "What's all this?"

A tentative smile curved his mouth. "I brought

you your magical Christmas. I remembered that you wanted snow."

Her jaw dropped. "How did you make it snow?"

He looked sheepish and gestured to the flakes still falling outside. "It's artificial snow—mostly water, but a few other things thrown in to keep it from melting quickly. A pilot friend of mine has a plane with a sprayer. He did me a favor."

She was flattered by the attention and all the trouble he'd gone to, but she couldn't forget what he'd done to her. "Why would you do that for me?"

His jaw hardened and he looked almost...frightened. Much like the way she felt when she looked out over a steep drop. "Because...I love you, Vee."

Her heart vaulted. She wanted to believe him. "Dominick, you don't have to say that—"

"I'm not just saying it, Vee. I mean it." He expelled a long, noisy breath. "I promised a wise woman once that if I ever met someone who made me feel more alive than the crazy stunts I've pulled, that I would jump."

She held her breath. Could it be true? She hadn't imagined the connection they'd shared?

Dominick looked utterly defeated. "I didn't mean for it to happen like this. Serves me right, I guess, for thinking I'd have fun teaching you a thing or two." He reached out and picked up her hand. "Instead, you taught me a thing or two." He kissed her fingers.

She was holding back tears, happy ones this time.

"Can you ever forgive me, Vee? Can you ever feel about me the way that I feel about you?"

Violet wet her lips, tasted tears. She nodded. "Yes."

He pulled her into his arms and crushed her against him, then sighed in her ear. "Thank you. Because I've got this bad feeling that I can't live without you."

She held him tighter, almost afraid to let go. He rocked her back and forth and she felt his love enveloping her, fortifying her.

"You know…" he murmured in a teasing voice "…if you want to stay with the whole exciting sex theme, I saw an elevator on the way in that has our name written all over it. I'm just saying."

Violet laughed and pulled back. Dominick's deep blue eyes reflected an emotion she'd never seen in them before—reciprocal, crazy romantic love.

It gave her a wondrous peek into the rest of her life.

Epilogue

"LOOK WHAT CAME in the mail today." Lillian Tremble held up a letter as she walked in.

Dr. Michelle Alexander glanced up from her computer. "What is it?"

"A letter from Violet Summerlin."

Michelle smiled. "What does she have to say?"

Lillian slit open the envelope and pulled out the letter. "'Dear Dr. Alexander, a few months ago I received the letter I wrote as an assignment in your Sexual Psyche class in college. Little did I know that it would set in motion a chain reaction of events that would bring about a life change—not only have I discovered the woman I think I was meant to be all along, but I also found the man of my dreams. We're going to be married soon, but I wanted to take time out from planning our adventure wedding to say thank you for your wisdom. This might sound a little strange, but for me, the timing of receiving my letter was almost magical. I never imagined I could be this happy. Warmest wishes, Violet Summerlin.'"

Lillian looked up from the letter and sighed. "Sounds like another success story."

Michelle turned to retrieve a thick black binder from the shelf behind her desk. "You met them both. Do you think they'll make it?"

"Oh, absolutely. Just like the others. Your sixth sense hasn't been wrong yet, sis."

Michelle found Violet's name in the binder and made a few notes.

"So—" Lillian sat on the corner of the desk. "Who's next?"

Michelle swiveled in her chair, pulled out a deep file bin and stared in at the hundreds and hundreds of envelopes containing letters written by former students of her Sex for Beginners class. She laid her hands on top of the pile and closed her eyes to listen. Which of her former students was in the most pain, which one faced the greatest emotional need? "When one of my students calls out to me, I'll be there."

Lillian winked. "You mean, *we'll* be there."

* * * * *

Silhouette Desire kicks off 2009 with
MAN OF THE MONTH, *a yearlong program*
featuring incredible heroes by stellar authors.

When navy SEAL Hunter Cabot returns home
for some much-needed R & R, he discovers
he's a married man. There's just one problem:
he's never met his "bride."

Enjoy this sneak peek at Maureen Child's
AN OFFICER AND A MILLIONAIRE.
Available January 2009 from Silhouette Desire.

One

Hunter Cabot, Navy SEAL, had a healing bullet wound in his side, thirty days' leave and, apparently, a wife he'd never met.

On the drive into his hometown of Springville, California, he stopped for gas at Charlie Evans's service station. That's where the trouble started.

"Hunter! Man, it's good to see you! Margie didn't tell us you were coming home."

"Margie?" Hunter leaned back against the front fender of his black pickup truck and winced as his side gave a small twinge of pain. Silently then, he watched as the man he'd known since high school filled his tank.

Charlie grinned, shook his head and pumped gas. "Guess your wife was lookin' for a little 'alone' time with you, huh?"

"My—" Hunter couldn't even say the word. *Wife?* He didn't have a wife. "Look, Charlie..."

"Don't blame her, of course," his friend said with a wink as he finished up and put the gas cap back on. "You being gone all the time with the SEALs must be hard on the ol' love life."

He'd never had any complaints, Hunter thought,

frowning at the man still talking a mile a minute. "What're you—"

"Bet Margie's anxious to see you. She told us all about that R and R trip you two took to Bali." Charlie's dark brown eyebrows lifted and wiggled.

"Charlie..."

"Hey, it's okay, you don't have to say a thing, man."

What the hell could he say? Hunter shook his head, paid for his gas and as he left, told himself Charlie was just losing it. Maybe the guy had been smelling gas fumes too long.

But as it turned out, it wasn't just Charlie. Stopped at a red light on Main Street, Hunter glanced out his window to smile at Mrs. Harker, his second-grade teacher who was now at least a hundred years old. In the middle of the crosswalk, the old lady stopped and shouted, "Hunter Cabot, you've got yourself a wonderful wife. I hope you appreciate her."

Scowling now, he only nodded at the old woman—the only teacher who'd ever scared the crap out of him. What the hell was going on here? Was everyone but him nuts?

His temper beginning to boil, he put up with a few more comments about his "wife" on the drive through town before finally pulling into the wide, circular drive leading to the Cabot mansion. Hunter didn't have a clue what was going on, but he planned to get to the bottom of it. Fast.

He grabbed his duffel bag, stalked into the house and paid no attention to the housekeeper, who ran at him, fluttering both hands. "Mr. Hunter!"

"Sorry, Sophie," he called out over his shoulder as he took the stairs two at a time. "Need a shower, then we'll talk."

He marched down the long, carpeted hallway to the rooms that were always kept ready for him. In his suite, Hunter tossed the duffel down and stopped dead. The shower in his bathroom was running. His *wife?*

Anger and curiosity boiled in his gut, creating a churning mass that had him moving forward without even thinking about it. He opened the bathroom door to a wall of steam and the sound of a woman singing—off-key. Margie, no doubt.

Well, if she was his wife... Hunter walked across the room, yanked the shower door open and stared in at a curvy, naked, temptingly wet woman.

She whirled to face him, slapping her arms across her naked body while she gave a short, terrified scream.

Hunter smiled. "Hi, honey. I'm home."

* * * * *

Be sure to look for
AN OFFICER AND A MILLIONAIRE
by USA TODAY bestselling author Maureen Child.
Available January 2009 from Silhouette Desire.

CELEBRATE
60 YEARS
OF PURE READING PLEASURE
WITH **HARLEQUIN**®!

**We'll be spotlighting a different series
every month throughout 2009
to celebrate our 60th anniversary.
Look for Silhouette Desire® in January!**

Collect all 12 books in the Silhouette Desire®
Man of the Month continuity, starting in
January 2009 with *An Officer and a Millionaire*
by *USA TODAY* bestselling author
Maureen Child.

*Look for one new Man of the Month title
every month in 2009!*

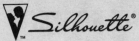

Silhouette®

Romantic
SUSPENSE

**Sparked by Danger,
Fueled by Passion.**

Justine Davis

Baby's Watch

THE COLTONS
~FAMILY FIRST~

Former bad boy Ryder Colton has never felt a
connection to much, so he's shocked when he feels
one to the baby he helps deliver, and her mother.
Ana Morales doesn't quite trust this stranger, but
when her daughter is taken by a smuggling ring,
she teams up with him in the hope of rescuing her
baby. With nowhere to turn she has no choice but
to trust Ryder with her life...and her heart.

Available January 2009 wherever books are sold.

Look for the final installment of
the Coltons: Family First miniseries,
A Hero of Her Own by Carla Cassidy in February 2009.

REQUEST YOUR FREE BOOKS!

2 FREE NOVELS PLUS 2 FREE GIFTS!

Red-hot reads!

YES! Please send me 2 FREE Harlequin® Blaze™ novels and my 2 FREE gifts (gifts are worth about $10). After receiving them, if I don't wish to receive any more books, I can return the shipping statement marked "cancel". If I don't cancel, I will receive 6 brand-new novels every month and be billed just $4.24 per book in the U.S. or $4.71 per book in Canada, plus 25¢ shipping and handling per book and applicable taxes, if any*. That's a savings of 15% or more off the cover price! I understand that accepting the 2 free books and gifts places me under no obligation to buy anything. I can always return a shipment and cancel at any time. Even if I never buy another book, the two free books and gifts are mine to keep forever.

151 HDN ERVA 351 HDN ERUX

Name	(PLEASE PRINT)	
Address		Apt. #
City	State/Prov.	Zip/Postal Code

Signature (if under 18, a parent or guardian must sign)

Mail to the Harlequin Reader Service:
IN U.S.A.: P.O. Box 1867, Buffalo, NY 14240-1867
IN CANADA: P.O. Box 609, Fort Erie, Ontario L2A 5X3

Not valid to current subscribers of Harlequin Blaze books.

Want to try two free books from another line?
Call 1-800-873-8635 or visit www.morefreebooks.com.

---

* Terms and prices subject to change without notice. N.Y. residents add applicable sales tax. Canadian residents will be charged applicable provincial taxes and GST. Offer not valid in Quebec. This offer is limited to one order per household. All orders subject to approval. Credit or debit balances in a customer's account(s) may be offset by any other outstanding balance owed by or to the customer. Please allow 4 to 6 weeks for delivery. Offer available while quantities last.

Your Privacy: Harlequin Books is committed to protecting your privacy. Our Privacy Policy is available online at www.eHarlequin.com or upon request from the Reader Service. From time to time we make our lists of customers available to reputable third parties who may have a product or service of interest to you. If you would prefer we not share your name and address, please check here. ☐

HB08R

Inside ROMANCE

Stay up-to-date on all your romance reading news!

The Inside Romance newsletter is a FREE quarterly newsletter highlighting our upcoming series releases and promotions!

Click on the <u>Inside Romance</u> link on the front page of **www.eHarlequin.com** or e-mail us at insideromance@harlequin.ca to sign up to receive your FREE newsletter today!

You can also subscribe by writing us at: HARLEQUIN BOOKS Attention: Customer Service Department P.O. Box 9057, Buffalo, NY 14269-9057

Please allow 4-6 weeks for delivery of the first issue by mail.

IRNBPA208

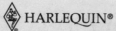

HARLEQUIN®

Blaze™

COMING NEXT MONTH

#441 EVERY BREATH YOU TAKE... Hope Tarr
Undercover FBI agent Cole Whittaker never has trouble putting his life on the line...but his heart? He almost lost it once, five years ago, and he's not chancing it again. Until he takes on a security job—to guard the one woman he's never been able to forget...

#442 LONE STAR SURRENDER Lisa Renee Jones
Rebellious undercover agent Constantine Vega takes D.A. Nicole Ward on the sexiest ride of her life as he protects her from a vengeful enemy—but who will protect her from him?

#443 NAKED AMBITION Jule McBride
J. D. Johnson's ambition is twofold: reclaim the life that once fed his soul as a successful country musician, and win back his small-town Southern belle. Only, Susannah's been kicking up her heels in NYC. Good thing J.D. knows all the right moves....

#444 NO HOLDING BACK Isabel Sharpe
24 Hours: Lost, Bk. 2
Reporter Hannah O'Reilly will do most anything for a story—including gate-crashing reclusive millionaire Jack Battle's estate on a stormy New Year's Eve. But as the snow piles up and sexy Jack starts making his moves, Hannah is achingly aware there's no holding back....

#445 A FEW GOOD MEN Tori Carrington
Uniformly Hot!/Encounters
Four soldiers, four destinies, four complete short stories! While on a tour of duty, Eric, Matt, Eddie and Brian have become a family. Only now, on their way home from Iraq, they have no idea what—or *who*—awaits them....

#446 AFTER DARK Wendy Etherington
"Irresistible" is how Sloan Caldwell describes Aidan Kendrick. The reclusive millionaire mogul may seem a lone wolf, but Sloan's sirenlike sensuality will soon change his ways....